Caraganis, Lynn.

Garish days

$15.45

GARISH DAYS

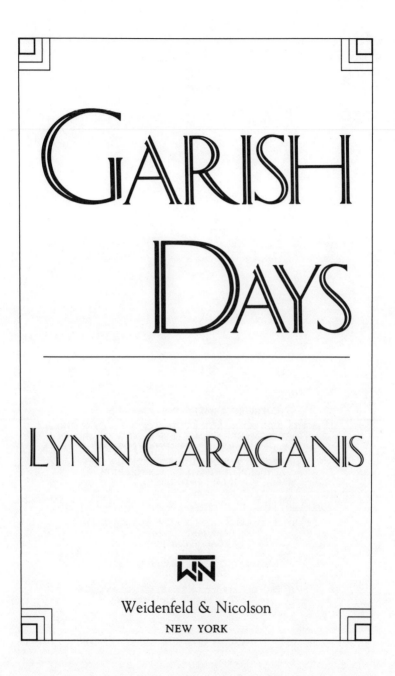

GARISH DAYS

LYNN CARAGANIS

Weidenfeld & Nicolson

NEW YORK

PUBLISHED BY WEIDENFELD & NICOLSON, NEW YORK
A DIVISION OF WHEATLAND CORPORATION
10 EAST 53RD STREET
NEW YORK, NY 10022

PUBLISHED IN CANADA BY GENERAL PUBLISHING COMPANY, LTD.

LIBRARY OF CONGRESS CATALOGING-IN-PUBLICATION DATA
CARAGANIS, LYNN.
GARISH DAYS.
I. TITLE.
PS3553.A637G3 1988   813'.54   87-8293
ISBN 1-55584-037-X

MANUFACTURED IN THE UNITED STATES OF AMERICA
DESIGNED BY RONNIE ANN HERMAN
FIRST EDITION
10 9 8 7 6 5 4 3 2 1

To the memory of
Luis Sanjurjo

GARISH DAYS

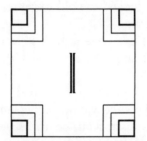

I AM NOT going to pretend that hordes of my contemporaries urged me to write this memoir.

My first important party was on a Saturday in February 1936. I was employed making hats at the Irving Hulder Company at that time—my first job. I left work at six on Friday. I had heard about a retail shop around Thirty-third Street that was undergoing liquidation, and I hurried over there to get myself some nice material for a dress. I remember I saw a rat in that shop running along the wall, which was a surprise, considering the racket and confusion of the sale. I found some taffetas, which I have always loved, and I was especially attracted to the black taffeta—but my mother would never have let me go in black, since I was only seventeen. The styles in those days were for an elegant nipped-in look—so there was really no use for taffeta, anyway. I noticed that the style of those days was captured perfectly in *The Great Ziegfeld*, on that actress with the lovely little nose, Myrna Loy.

With difficulty I resisted the emerald-green taffeta and settled on some nice yellow satin—not too bright. I got four yards for three dollars and fifty cents. I looked carefully at the cashier to see if she was dreading liquidation, but I saw no sign of it. Yet she looked too old to get another job. Possibly she was able to retire.

When everyone had gone to bed, I cleared the newspapers off the table and I laid out my fabric. I always sew without a pattern—merely take a good long stare before I cut. I worked till one or two that morning and I had a nice dress in time for the party. The bodice was perfectly plain and loose fitting, which was the style, in addition to its being rather low. It was snug around the hips and hung four inches above the floor. The aim was to present yourself as a pristine goddess while artlessly showing your bosom. I wore my mother's seed-pearl necklace.

We lived at Seventieth Street and I took a taxicab downtown. The driver complained about the cold. I was wearing an old fur stole of my mother's—the wearing of furs now seems to me criminal. This cabdriver was from Canarsie, Brooklyn, and told me about his Italian bride who hadn't yet arrived in this country. He wasn't Italian, but he liked Italians. When we pulled up to the place and I was still inside, a man dashed out and claimed the cab. The driver said, "Hold your horses, Jake." I let him keep the change, for luck.

I left my stole with an old lady who sat dozing by the coatroom in a frilly white apron. I then went directly to the ladies' dressing room, simply to display a nice compact, I'm afraid. The way our hair was then—flat waves jammed down on your head—nothing could dislodge it. In the midst of all those dressed-up women, my outfit began to look less striking than it had at home. But I guess I powdered away undaunted.

There was a narrow, long hallway paneled in oak, and I made my way along this with a shoal of other women, chatting in pairs or solitary, like myself. I had a black satin evening bag over my shoulder on a chain.

The room where the party was going on had dark walls and was lighted up with chandeliers. There was a long buffet table on one side, but there were waiters, too, to bring your drinks. One came to me right away and I took a glass from him, but I had promised not to drink. A group of five young men stood in conversation perhaps twelve feet away, and one of them kept looking up at me. I would glance away and look around the room. Soon he came over to me. If I had to describe his looks, I would say he was between handsome and plain. He was dark and medium-sized. I thought he was fairly attractive.

"Well, *you're* young," he said to me. "Did your mother let you out?"

I was determined to make the fellow understand how clumsy I found these remarks, so I stared at him and then said slowly, "Did my mother let me out?"

He brushed ashes off his shirtfront and then said, "Yes," falsely jaunty. "Want a drink? Oh, I see you've got one."

"How old might *you* be, then?" I said.

"Sorry," he said in a vague, formal voice. "I've just seen someone," and he hurried away.

I might as well say I had no more interesting conversations that evening. I ate salmon and a type of scalloped potatoes with pimento. I remember I satisfied myself that I was the tallest woman there. A red-haired man had an argument with a red-haired woman near the middle of the room, which drew the party together for the few minutes till they both rushed out. One man had a beard—a great curiosity for those times—and someone pointed out Cordell Hull.

At midnight I went home in a cab. I was pleased overall, and that was my first party. I describe it at length because it was my first, and parties are what I have loved most my whole

5

life. I worked at the Irving Hulder Company until April that year and left it when I could, because I had no interest in hats. I then went to work at Lazarus's, and eventually I was sent by them to Europe. That was the real beginning of my memories, in spite of what I've just written as a pretext for telling about the rat.

I went in August 1938. *Thinking* people knew what was going on in Europe but I wasn't one of them. I was in a fool's paradise, but it ended quickly and I learned my lesson along with the rest of the world.

I was sent to Europe to look, but privately I also felt it necessary I be looked at. I'm always struck by that Cardinal Newman lyric where he says scornfully "I loved the garish day." Meaning he wanted to be in the spotlight. But it's a harmless desire! If more people felt it there'd be more fun in the world. More fun, more costume parties, and fewer wars. You see, I sympathize with that rat, who ran out into the bright lights to "mix" and be seen. It's the backroom boys I don't trust.

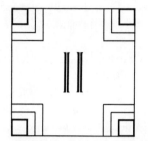

II

MY MOTHER and father did not want to hear about my going to Europe. That some might be forced to travel to get or keep a job they could comprehend, but those things— in their view—could not apply to me. My brilliance and cour- age had been legendary ever since, according to a prized family story, I had let go my mother's hand and run away into the classroom alone on my first day of school. That I might want to travel for the sake of seeing things did not enter their minds, especially as, to take my job at Lazarus's, I'd already moved to Ohio.

My mother proposed I stay on in Ohio a little longer before letting myself be "forced" to go. When I explained the ad- vantages of my going, she tried to cry a little bit and appear old. Then she went out of the room and came back in with her stole wrapped in tissue paper. Suddenly casual, she offered it to me, whether as a bribe or some kind of pledge I don't know. My father looked on pleasantly, as if the matter was now settled.

But by now I saw it for the poor rag it was. Even at that time I disliked the idea of the animal's being made to bite its own tail and stare throughout eternity. I said something like "I could never take it!" and easily persuaded her to wrap it up again. As she did so she said, "You're going. I see that now."

My father said, "First Ohio, now Europe," and he shook his head over my originality.

Of course there was no family party for my going, but Lazarus's did give me one. It was on August 26, a Friday, the night before I left Ohio. My boss—who was my aunt Hattie— gave the party and Mr. Lazarus came by—I suppose because it happened to be held in the reception room outside his office. For all I knew he was just passing through on his way home to dinner. I imagine he had barely heard of me, though he certainly knew somebody was going to Paris. When he came by, Hattie saw to it that he stopped. Very showily he came over and shook me by the hand and said a few suitable things. He was a big, bald man who dressed beautifully, and would listen attentively without leaning forward, which was very dignified. He looked over my clothes and said that he was certain I knew my business and would be very sharp over there.

During this Hattie bobbed up and down and beamed, as though Mr. Lazarus and I were just two of her rising protégés. Hattie had a collection of small felt hats that she pinned to the side of her head and wore all day at the store and perhaps at home with her bathrobe. I always found these comical. However competent and talented she was, she looked foolish—like a rural woman from somewhere, something like Ma Kettle. And Hattie always ridiculed my taste in shoes, in which she claimed to see signs of wantonness, because I always wore high heels, even in blizzards.

After meeting me Mr. Lazarus turned away. Rather than

8

leave the party at this point, he went and sat down by himself and attracted no more attention than if he had been a waiter.

Hattie had thoughtfully invited a friend of mine who was a salesclerk in shoes and handbags. I don't know how Hattie knew I knew her. Her name was Betty Wheeler. We had met at the streetcar stop. Betty always meant to quit Lazarus's; she "hated retail." But nobody quit in those days.

Betty lived with her father. He was a busted farmer. They lived in a tenement, and he didn't let her buy a thing. All he wanted was to find a wife and get married. She told me they used to go to agricultural fairs in every part of Ohio, so he could just walk up and down the booths to look for women he might like. When he found one, Betty would have to go strike up a conversation with her—then introduce her to the old man. She suffered the tortures of the damned with her father.

Betty had a dress made of chenille—the bedspread mate-rial—which had an effect on everybody who saw her. Not only because it looked strange, but because it was associated in people's minds with beds. "Oh, hell," she would say wearily when some stranger would begin to peer at her. Betty happened to be wearing her chenille dress on the day of the party, so she stood right behind me and it was hard to talk to her.

The three women's-wear buyers were present, most of whom were suspicious of me because of my sudden appearance and sudden rise through the ranks. But I was Hattie's, and they were wary of crossing her.

We drank champagne out of what must have been Lazarus-family crystal, or such as might have been used in toasts with Mr. Wanamaker and Mr. Filene; this and other things have made me wonder since if there wasn't something personal between Mr. Lazarus and Hattie. We drank plenty of cham-pagne and Hattie and I made a lot of noise laughing, but most of the guests disliked me. They would approach me in that melodramatic way men suppose women behave toward each other and which you so often see on the stage, looking each other up and down as if to see whether they can "keep a man." These women slithered around my party like this, even a fat, elderly one, but only because they were so controlled by men's ideas. All were obliged to congratulate me, of course. I demonstrated my own maturity by winking over their shoulders at Hattie and eventually by winking in their faces.

I kept trying to say things to Betty, but she kept moving out of reach. Then Hattie made a speech about my trip. She began by telling them how she had "found" me—the daughter of her "oldest friend" (actually, her brother, my father), who had hinted to her that I had "commercial talent and determination—having sewed all my own clothes since the age of two." No one could have believed this and yet no one laughed, except of course Hattie and me. She went on to say that my father had denied everything when he found out she meant to hire me away to Columbus, because I was the "prop" of my small family. This was also not true. Then she described the bold commercial ideas that had occurred to me during my months as her assistant—candlelight in the French Room!— and how in me she had discovered a mind that was "truly retail to its finger ends." She said I was certain to use my time in Paris to very good advantage because, though new to the company, I felt Lazarus's was really my new home—a thing I had never said. Then she briskly added that I was sure to attract a good deal of attention over there on account of my shoes. The buyers stared at my feet and turned over the question of whether to laugh, then digested it without a murmur, so that once again it was just Hattie and me. She closed her speech by repeating my work motto—actually, her work motto— telling the group that I had the old ideals of "honesty, industry and a hard right to the button." Betty thought she was insulting me.

I publicly thanked Hattie for her confidence and I thanked Mr. Lazarus, who was still with us. Then, just to tease her, I thanked Betty Wheeler, which caused the whole party—once and for all—to turn and get a good look at her chenille dress. While she blushed and nodded, I felt sorry I'd done it. I took her hand and told them Betty had had nothing to do with my shoe wardrobe. This made them laugh angrily—they took it for another in-joke, but they would have understood it if they had not been too arrogant to recognize the clerks and know what departments they belonged to.

They all left after my speech—not troubling to say *bon voyage* to me. Then Betty and I rushed up and down the table emptying plates of fish-paste sandwiches and "cheese dreams" and drunkenly wrapping them in white damask napkins, while Mr. Lazarus and Hattie chatted together. We shoved these bundles into the pockets of our dresses and into our purses— then I walked with dignity over to where Hattie stood by Mr. Lazarus's chair. He shook my hand nicely once more. Then I shook hands with Hattie, brought Betty forward so that Mr. Lazarus might remember her face, then the two of us ran out, spurning the private elevator in favor of the dirty stairs. We sat in the trolley and opened all our bundles and offered them to each other. I remember I told Betty she should try to leave Columbus for New York right away, and she told me it was better to stay in one place and not get "too smart." As I was drunk this made me thoughtful and sad for a few minutes. I always liked Betty Wheeler and I did not lose touch with her until the 1950s, when she moved to California, a well-to-do married woman.

11

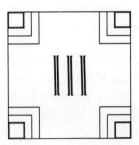

MY FATHER went with me to the boat while my mother stayed at home making herself surly with worry. She was an obdurate person, in contrast with my father, who forgot his own opinions from day to day.

In the taxi he stretched out all over the seat and said, "We only go to the West Side when we're on our way to Europe."

I was traveling on the *Berengaria*. My father stood patiently by me through the lines on both sides of the gangway—both lines turbulent with shouting people crisscrossing them, their suitcases held over their heads and their hats knocked off. Everybody on the pier was a madcap but the men who belonged to the ship—and the nicer their uniforms, the more statesmanlike and sad they appeared. One by one my father mistook these people for the captain, including the one who ran up and scrawled something on my baggage with a piece of chalk. When in strange surroundings it was always my father's way to exclaim at every novel thing, till wonderment overtook his faculties, and then he would exclaim at things he saw every day. He would start calling everybody sir. Maybe that's why he so seldom went out. He did not even go to work. He had decided that his income from a building he owned would be enough for us. He felt vindicated later on when men who still went to work couldn't make anything.

The metal corridors inside the ship were crowded with laughing men and women. Pouring and drinking and shouting were the only things, and also blocking the way of passengers, either because they liked them or because they didn't like them.

I put on a stern expression and made the opening for us, but my father followed slowly, because he wanted them to see how new he was to shipboard life, and be kind to him. He would have smiled and bowed himself into exhaustion if we had not reached my cabin when we did.

"Oh, my, look at the beds," he said in amazement. Then like a little old lady he crouched down to stack my cases, muttering anxiously and putting the small ones down first, the large ones on top of them. Then he pointed to a lower bunk.

"Do I sit here?" he said.

It was a second-class cabin—made for two. There were no windows. Through a door there was an elegant little bathroom. I sat myself on the sink and watched my father. I could not resist the happy mood of the people outside. My father would not sit back and rest, though. He sat staring at a spot on the floor, probably trying to think like a hayseed.

One of the holidaymakers tapped at the open door and entered, two of his friends standing beaming in at us from outside the doorway. He was a big, flushed young man. He held a flask up in the air and said, "Friends and fellow travelers—oh, excuse me!—I'm bringing you some liquor. When you are going on a trip, you have to be nice to each other—Americans always are!"

He paused to reach for the water glasses behind me, and I stood up as he ran his hand along my back. He blinked.

"Young lady! No harm done!" he said, and I laughed.

"We're well-meaning young American fellows, varsity fellows! Harmless youths. Working quietly for civilization!"

This old Prohibition joke brought my father to his feet and he shook the man's hand while the speech continued. "We're happy, you see. Well, if we can make the other fellow happy," he said, gesturing at my father and me, "what if we *be* strangers? What of that?"

I laughed at him, and as I did, he nodded pleasantly at me and poured whiskey into the bottom of our glasses. Then he shook hands with both of us and left, turning back suddenly at the door to bow. Then he turned again and, realizing his friends were gone, seemed anxious to come back in. At that moment I turned away and he left us.

"Jazz babies," said my father. "Did you see him? Generous, though." He filled the glasses from the sink and he handed me mine saying, "I'll finish that."

We both finished our own, and the squealing outside seemed to recede. My father returned to his usual faint pessimism. He said, "I hope this goes well for you. I hope it does. I've never had much faith in Hattie, you know that. When your mother and I were first married, sometime around then, you know, don't you, that she went out to Santa Fe and went Indian? She wouldn't answer letters. She tried to live in there among the squaws! When her money was gone, she came back out again. That was two days later. And yet supposedly they use the barter system."

Many's the time I've tried to imagine Hattie scrambling over the rocks in buckskins, and stopping to peer out over the prairie, a little hat trimmed with miniature corn on her head, or sitting in a circle of Indian women, teaching them how to choose scarves and jewelry to stretch their wardrobes.

Then my father said, "How 'bout Russia? You know there's just as much graft over there as they have over here, even with their system, and there's not a thing they can do to prevent it. It's human nature. Man's a beast, honey, and I'll say so till I'm blue in the face!"

"I'm not going over there, Dad."

"Don't you go there, dear," he said. "You look awfully good today. You're going to get proposals!" he said, suddenly hitting his knee with his fist. "But you'd be a fool to accept—I don't care *who* it may be. We live very well over here in this country, America. No more Ohio business, either. You'll come right back to us and . . . we'll do very well."

That maudlin feeling started to come over me again, as after I talked to Betty on the streetcar.

"How'd you like that whiskey? Ever had anything like that before? You're laughing for no reason—are you laughing?—so I guess you're one of those who haven't got a head for it. Better not drink over there. You can drink when you come back, though, *if* your mother and I are with you."

The steam whistle had been blowing on and off. My father spoke right through it, only frowning.

"He's a nice fellow, that jazz baby. I'll thank him when I go out. Don't you thank him. All ashore," he said. He slowly stood up and put on his hat. "What if I passed out and couldn't get off? Good Lord, I'd have to go with you!" He stepped into the corridor and turned back to tell me not to come with him and not to speak to the jazz baby out at sea. I did not go with him either, because I'd drunk a little too much.

I slept and woke up to the whistle blowing and the throbbing sound coming through my pillow. I threw cold water on my face and fixed my hair. A letter from Hattie had been delivered while I slept. I put it in my pocket. I was in too much haste to see us leave the harbor and see everybody wave.

The corridors were empty and I didn't see a soul until I got out on deck. I stood by the railing in the stern and looked across at the city and the small red ship that marked the way into the harbor. This ship was called the *Ambrose*, and everybody who sailed in or out of New York knew it. Once, I think, it was cut in two by an ocean liner in a fog, because the captains always steered right at it.

Between our ship and the *Ambrose* stretched the green wake. It looked so much like a sidewalk that several times I had the impulse to get down and run back to say good-bye, though I didn't know any of the harbor men on board. I was feeling, as we steamed away, that all New York people were kind and good-hearted, all baseball fans with names like Hank and Judy and Buddy. I wanted to stay with them and not face the toreadors and stuffed-shirt men I felt were looming up on the other side, busy brushing off their tuxedos and preparing remarks like "*Mademoiselle* is so charmingly naïve!" and, "You American designers all come to Paris to learn tailoring!"

These thoughts made me uncomfortable. I didn't want to look anymore. I remembered Hattie's letter, so I took it out and read it.

Dear Honeybunch,

Before I leave for home I'll just write you a little note. I'll mail it to 81st Street and then maybe you'll get it before you leave.

Gert just came in to close the windows but I told her not to! This weather reminds me of the old days back on the Little Muddy. We used to take off all our clothes and put on our hats and go lie out under a hackberry tree, where it wasn't a bit cooler than anywhere else. Just an old Spanish custom, I guess. Maybe you and I'll take a trip out that way in the spring. See the prickly pears. Would you like to?

Just had our monthly meeting with the gay Lutherans from the accounting section. These meetings always make me want to shut myself up away somewhere with nothing but my banjo. I believe I'm ready to sit down and learn "Old Zip Coon" right through. You know how long I've been working on that one.

Poor Mr. Lazarus can't get a minute's relief and he won't go on vacation. He says he's afraid if he left town I'd close down the appliance department and put out more clothes.

I was telling him he's mighty lucky he has so many dependable people around him—*including* a brilliant young woman to go to Paris for him. "Now just how is that, Hattie?" he says. "Is it so hard to find young women willing to go to Paris and look at clothes all day without a care in the world?" He tries to get a rise out of me, but he can't.

Remember, don't you worry!

Love, Hattie

It was just the thing to make me feel worse.

I chased the steward and asked him for something to drink. He directed me indoors, where through the glass I could see some people standing close together around a bar. I made my way through them, and when the bartender looked up at me, I ordered a ginger ale. There was a silence after this, which probably had nothing to do with me, but I suddenly added, "With whiskey!" Then before I knew it, everybody was shouting with laughter, and I laughed, too.

In the midst of all this roaring, I fixed my eyes on the steward who was mixing it, trying to tell from his expression whether what I had ordered was a real drink. In fact he poured bourbon in, not whiskey, and I'm sure he did it out of kindness.

The other people had resumed their chattering. I was entirely hemmed in by people beside and behind me, and I didn't know any of them.

Next to me sat a small woman wearing a white beret studded with rhinestones. She nodded her head as she talked, and I watched the back of her hat. Then she turned and looked into her bag, rattling through her cases till she found a cigarette. The steward gave her a light and as she turned toward him, I heard her say to the person on the other side, "One of those Miss Noli Me Tangeres—you know what I mean. In a big, stiff organdy blouse with a bow!"

The steward asked me if I was on a pleasure trip, and someone put his mouth up to my ear and whispered "New in town?"

This was the jazz baby, with a contented expression on his face.

"How are you?" I said, twisting around to look at his red skin and yellow hair (in spite of which he was attractive).

"I hope the old gentleman didn't leave the ship on my account. He didn't misunderstand my visit, did he?" he said with a sigh. "One minute you are so happy together in your snug cabin with your little pile of luggage. Next minute he's shuffling away like a broken man. He thanked me, though. It was beautiful and poignant. He asked me to keep an eye on you—imagine!—and I agreed!"

All this the jazz baby said fluently, with a sincere expression on his face, as if he believed my father was my brokenhearted old boyfriend.

"Well, you don't have to worry about him. He has another girl at home."

"He was a broken man, I tell you," he said, laying a hand on my shoulder for emphasis.

"Where are the other varsity men?"

18

"Why, here's one of them," he said, and touched the shoulder of the woman next to me.

"Hello," she said and peered up at him. "Where've you been?" Then she looked at me and smiled.

"Jean, this is my little American friend," he said, indicating me. "Jean is my wife."

"Aren't you American?" I asked, and the jazz baby said, "We *were*, but now we're moving to Europe, and these are the sorts of things I'm going to say over there."

As he spoke, he stood between us with a hand on each of our shoulders, and he had twisted us so that we would both be looking right at him. Suddenly he turned away and cried out, "Harry!" and left us.

His wife laughed and said, "Isn't he common?" She had frizzy auburn hair tucked under her hat, and a pale white face. She asked me if I wanted another drink. I was ready, in a way, but I said no because the walls and people were moving upward together and I had a vision of that continuing through the whole voyage—seven days or whatever it was—and of there being a scandal for Lazarus's when I was carried off at Cherbourg.

"Traveling for pleasure?" said a man's voice from the other side. I turned. He was a white-haired, middle-aged man. He was looking at me earnestly.

"No," I said in a stern voice, trying to suggest that in the circumstances it was no use trying to get any fun out of me.

"I have to work, too. I'm a doctor," he said.

Then the girl in the beret brought her head down near my shoulder on the other side and whispered, "I'm a *doctor*. Servant of mankind!"

I thought this was almost unbelievably funny and I remember us both screaming. I don't know whether the doctor heard, or what he thought.

Then the jazz baby, whose name was Ed, came back and took us to dinner.

I was seated far from them at a table with three people I of course didn't know, and though we were table mates all through the voyage, I don't remember them at all. The dining room was beautiful—really beautiful—though in a Spartan way. I'll never understand how they kept the linens blinding white with never any spots! The glasses always gleamed, and the fresh fruit was lovely to the end of the voyage. These things alone could account for the great affection these ships, and especially the Cunard and White Star ships, inspired in everybody.

We had Smithfield ham, cold roast beef, potato, asparagus-tip salad, coffee and trifle, and we all ate like wild pigs. At least that is my impression. Outside the windows it was pitch-dark and it really shocked me to think that we were out at sea, far from everything. Because even though I had left my family and moved to Ohio to take a job, I knew I was still the biggest baby in the world.

IWOKE UP late next day—too late to get breakfast. I just lay there and tried to believe I was shooting along underwater, and wished I had a porthole. If I had, I now know it would only have looked in on some other person lying in a bunk. Then I noticed a package on the floor, so I jumped down.

It was to me from Brentano's, Booksellers to the World, according to the wrapper. The thought crossed my mind that an embittered German immigrant might have put it there, after putting a bomb in it. I tell this to show our foolish thinking about the Germans as late as 1938. We all despised Hitler, but that was about all there was to it. And then we had the idea, unconnected to Hitler, that certain Germans wanted to "sabotage" us. Embittered or unemployed Germans might want to set New York piers on fire, just as cheerful Germans might want to drink beer, but it was viewed as an individual thing. Perhaps it got going when Bruno Richard

21

Hauptmann was arrested and then electrocuted, after a ridiculous trial.

We, I mean the people I knew, didn't put two and two together until it was pathetically late. Of course I sympathize with the desire not to see a war coming. I found this passage in the Germany section of my Fodor's travel book for that year.

UNIFORMS

It certainly seems a fact that the Germans love uniforms and are proud of being able to wear them. This, however, has nothing to do with the militarism of old times—it is a leaning toward voluntary organization and discipline which to us English seems strange and hard to understand, though there is no reason why we should grudge others a pleasure we do not covet ourselves. Especially when a love of uniform is combined with a love of peace, as in the case of my neighbor, the friendly jeweler who declared in every second sentence that no one in Germany desires war.

Then he says,

I realized, however, that the question of where I should stay in Cologne was a more interesting and important one than that of politics.

I love that one.

During that crossing Jean told me she had first made reservations on the *Europa*. The office she called was in Manhattan, but the man answered the phone by saying "Heil Hitler" instead of hello. To us it was funny, just clownish, and the switch to our ship had nothing to do with Hitler;

they changed because Ed heard the German ships had march-
ing bands and exercising.

Anyway, I was not a victim of sabotage. Inside the package
I found five or six books, and a card with the best wishes of
F. Lazarus, Mr. Lazarus himself. How amazed Betty would
have been to see it. I would have been, too, if the books had
not all been by Fannie Hurst, Hattie's personal idol.

I can see her so well in my mind as she would have stood
there beside the seated Mr. Lazarus, beaming and telling him
how much his signature would mean to me, and holding the
little card up against her chest and looking sideways at him,
so disarming in her hat.

I find it very hard to believe that she is dead, and yet it's
been almost thirty years since I saw her walking around. I'd
never thought that Hattie might die. For years I went on
thinking, "I must tell Hattie" or "I'll find out from Hattie."
Even now I can't help wondering what she'd say to me about
my life if she were here.

I unpacked and put away my clothes, worried that I wouldn't
have enough. I had to visit four shows in Paris—Patou and
Schiaparelli, Chanel and Balmain. For these I had brought a
dressy black suit by Augustabernard, as well as some awkwardly
high shoes. I had a demure long dressy dress made of pale blue
wool shantung—a copy—that I meant to wear out in the
evenings, though I did not know if, as representing Lazarus's
but being nobody in my own right, I would be invited everywhere or ignored, and I didn't care. I suppose I knew I would
go out anyway. I had also brought slacks, not realizing that
they would attract too much attention and be useless.

Then in a cumbersome box I had two hats—not those Robin
Hood caps, but hats with wide brims. Hanging in the little
closet was my white wool coat—they called it "dead white"
in those days—for which I'd had to stand firm while all the

experts in Coats and Suits and Better Dresses bore down on me. White was a ridiculous choice for traveling at any time, they explained. And this was the wrong season for it. Did I want to go over there and look flashy? Did I realize I would look like Carmen Miranda over there among those rich women from ancient families who dominated the fashion industry? They would think I was "another Wally Simpson" and despise me. I would end up hurting the reputation of Lazarus's instead of enhancing it, which was what they were sending me to do, as they hoped I certainly understood. But I didn't yield. When I was over there, I saw the Norman Hartnell coat that must have been the original, though that version had absurd buttons. I wore my coat till it was in pieces and then had another one made exactly like it but about a foot longer because that was 1957.

I dressed and went out, climbing the many staircases to the deck. The air was mild—it was mild and cloudy during all of that voyage. The green wake still preserved itself all the way to the horizon, but now there was no red *Ambrose* at the other end. There was nothing anywhere but clouds and waves. If you have never been on the ocean, you may not realize it, but that's all there is. And the clouds and waves give you an impression of strength and meaninglessness combined. That is what makes it exciting and strange. A clean white tablecloth becomes a poignant object! In the back of your mind, you know that, comfortable as you are, if the ship should disappear, you'd be freezing and sinking, or half-eaten by a shark. You put aside these thoughts, but they come back, sometimes as fellow feeling for objects—especially things like clean tablecloths or fussy lampshades like those in the dining room. Suddenly you imagine you are seeing it in tatters, plowing through the water on the nose of a shark, then pulled to ribbons by big crabs on the bottom.

That morning Jean called to me from a chair drawn up with all the others against what we called the wheelhouse, for some reason, and presented me with the chair next to her. Ed had reserved it for me and it was mine—a valuable favor because by this time all the chairs were spoken for and I would have been doomed to standing at the rail or sitting alone inside and never getting into any clique.

There was a girl like that, a girl of about my age who had no chair. She wore a bulgy knit suit and she just walked to and fro. I saw her urging a steward in a low voice to get her a drink. He refused and she said, "You goddamn gyp' " in a low voice. She used to sit in any vacant chair, but this never gave her more than a few minutes' peace before the steward would see its real owner coming and she would have to get up, which she did with bad grace and only at the last minute.

Nobody knew why she was not allowed to have a drink, but there was something about her that made you sure it was her own fault. Everyone but her had a chair, too, and anyone could get a chair. We knew this because we all had them.

I remember Ed's friend Harry saying that since she only had one outfit, she must have come to this ship straight from jail. Pretty soon we all called her "the Bolshie." We joked about how if we ever had to abandon ship, she would get a lifeboat all to herself and row away as fast as she could, then sink it out of spite before our eyes. We didn't speak to her, we only gawked at her.

I gladly took my chair, unfolded the plaid blanket and pulled it over me, then right away felt restless.

"You don't need that," said Jean. "Steward," she called happily, and when the steward came and stood by us she said excitedly, "Guess what we want this morning? A gin fizz."

"Very good," he said. He was amused by Jean.

"Not for me," I said. "Do you really want a drink now?"

"*I* don't, but he does," she said, pointing at her stomach.

"Who?"

"And what will *you* have, miss?"

"Have bouillon," said Jean. "Bouillon," she told the steward.

"I'm pregnant," she said when he had gone away. I know I was so inexperienced that all I could think of, looking at her pale face, was maternity dresses at Lazarus's, which Hattie called "bladder tops."

So I said, "Does it show?"

"It depends on . . . depends on—well, I don't know," she said. "I get the feeling it's a very *small* baby." For a second we just stared at her stomach.

"This is why we're going to Europe," she said. "We're going to live off my parents. They don't know about this little thing," she said, pointing again. "They don't know about that big thing either," she said, waving her arm vaguely around the deck, meaning Ed, I guess. "Up till this I've been an angel. I went to Simmons College! So."

The steward came back with our drinks. I drank my bouillon and she drank her gin. She said, "I'm a bit sick, aren't you? But this helps."

"Looking at your drink might make me sick," I told her.

She said, "That's funny, because I don't like bouillon."

So we sat all wrapped up in the open air watching the sea and the sporty groups around the deck.

"Ed and Harry are over there playing ringtoss or something like big dolts. We don't really *know* Harry," she went on.

26

"Harry's a new friend from yesterday. He's very Lake Forest."

Soon Ed and Harry came sauntering along. Ed was saying, " 'Girls Girls Girls.' " This was part of a song he used to sing under his breath that went like this:

> Girls Girls Girls
> Big Girls Small Girls
> Any Girl's the right
> Girl for me.

During this song or whatever it was, he would illustrate by pointings and gestures, depending on how he felt. But except for me, Ed didn't flirt with anyone but Jean, and with Jean he behaved like a normal man in love.

Harry was presented to me, then sat down next to Jean. Ed sat down with me. He pretended the ship was his and asked me to tell him the name of any steward who wasn't nice to me, and promised to "beat the crap" out of him. This was funny because of the way the stewards all radiated kindness as well as courtesy, which Ed didn't.

Then a squat old woman in a blue suit with a bertha and plenty of jewelry pounded toward us along the deck, her purse held in two hands tight across her stomach. She made so much noise we all looked at her shoes, which were stodgy things like bricks. At the crown, flaps of leather stood up like wings. She came to a stop and demanded that Ed give up his chair. She said it was her chair.

"I know it's your chair," he said exaggeratedly. He got up and took Harry's chair, and Harry sat down at Jean's feet, facing me.

"Pretty loathsome," he said, meaning the old woman. "I wonder they let it circulate. Ought to be tied down somewhere. Tie her to the mast or something."

Ed leaned forward and said to me, "Harry played ringtoss at Yale."

"I *did* go to Yale, matter of fact," said Harry in surprise.

"Hooray!" said Jean.

"What year, Harry?" said Ed.

" 'Thirty-seven."

"That's my year. NYU. The Fighting Catholics. No, the Bulldogs!"

Harry grimaced.

"So, Harry," Ed went on, "did you by any chance come down at Thanksgiving for the riot last year?"

"I did. It was pretty loathsome."

"You're telling me."

"I don't remember a thing till the conductor shook me up in New Haven," Harry said.

"I remember my heart used to go pit-a-pat when I got to New Haven on the train, but that was a long time ago," said Jean.

"That so?" said Harry proudly.

Ed laughed. Then he suddenly took Jean's hand. "Look along there past the woman in the white thing," he said, steering her around. "See that fellow in the spats?"

"Those aren't spats," Jean said.

"Well, big socks." He laughed again. "You won't believe this! It's just unutterable."

We all leaned toward him.

"That fellow walked up to me this morning. I was just standing at the rail, and he started telling me about the weather and all, and it was too stupid to listen to." He demonstrated how he'd nodded his head like an imbecile. "He told me he was a doctor, and how he manages to operate in rough seas, because more people need operations when the sea is rough.

And then he turned to me and said, *'Ever been a fairy?'* Right out of the blue!"

We all shouted at this, but Harry made a loud snorting sound. He appeared to be laughing, but it was partly writhing.

"Who the blazes does he think I am?" said Jean.

"What about me?" said Ed.

Then in a loud, offensive voice the old woman next to me said, "What time's lunch around here?" She had just returned from walking around.

There was a second or two of quiet. Then Ed said, "You mean you didn't know you were supposed to bring your own lunch?"

She looked put out, and turned away and stared into her purse.

"See you later," said Harry quietly to me, and walked away.

"Harry's a real self-kidder," said Ed.

"Well, he's just so very Lake Forest," said Jean.

After luncheon I was seasick and I went straight back to my chair. Jean was there, asleep. I fell asleep, too, but then woke up. Ed was laughing loudly in his chair over a newspaper. He wanted to read it to me. I pointed out Jean, but he just waved that away and started reading. It was about one of the Rough Riders, now an old man. This man had shot and killed another man, because the man had said to him, "You think you're pretty tough, don't you?" Ed laughed over this for several minutes without stopping. Jean woke up. He was delighted and he read it over again to her. This time it seemed to strike him in some new way, as if it were a brand-new joke, and he laughed till he was an alarming deep red.

In the middle of this, a distinguished-looking steward in a beautiful uniform came and stood by my chair.

"Yes, how do you do, miss," he began. "A lady will be

moving into your cabin for the rest of the voyage. I hope this won't be disturbing to you. She's an elderly lady named Mrs. Trent."

"No, it's all right," I said, wondering.

"She has her key already, so please don't be alarmed when you go back."

I said thank you and he went away.

"Hard luck," said Jean.

I did wonder what this would mean but again fell asleep. It must have been the open air.

When I woke up, Ed was squeezed into Jean's chair holding her hand in his, his other arm around her shoulders. He had her laughing; he was saying things like "Give me a kiss right here and now, girlie."

"No," said Jean, laughing.

"You rich high-society women are all alike," said Ed.

"I'm not rich."

"She is," Ed said to me.

"She is?" I said.

"Are you kidding? Her father was the biggest crooked banker. . . . Once they saw him running down an alley, and it gave them the idea to start the SEC. Jean, tell her what he said when the bank collapsed."

"No," she screamed. "Get out of my chair."

"Just tell her. Go ahead, I—"

"He said, 'I was always an agrarian myself,' " said Jean, tired out and laughing between each word.

That night after dinner there was dancing. I danced with Ed, Harry and the doctor—but only briefly with the doctor, because Ed cut in on us. Ed also danced with "the old battle-ax," spending a long time away from the party to look for her. It was just something he got it into his head to do. He found her playing cards, in evening dress, matching turban and her wing shoes, in the library, and then for a while some of us also danced in the library, even though you couldn't hear the band in there.

Late in the evening I went out on deck, being drunk and getting into that phase when you say to yourself, "Why do I drink that stuff?" Harry came out with me. As I stared out at the sea thinking about myself, he stared at my profile.

"Tell me something," he said. "Is Ed as screwy as he seems?"

"I think so," I said. "Why ask me?"

"Why, all the women are nuts about him." Now he eased me around and we stared into each other's eyes. But I was still thinking about my own condition. All of a sudden then, he kissed me. I just shook him off, deciding then and there to go to my cabin where I could wash my face. I was too indifferent to Harry to enjoy kissing him.

I clattered my way down the strange corridors, the figure of my still-unseen cabinmate changing one sinister shape for another as I went. It *could* be the battle-ax. She was elderly. It would be somebody who had found fault with her first arrangements. A fussbudget of some kind. Or else she had been objected to because of a disease, or a habit of stealing, or of screaming in her sleep, or of staring at other people while *they* were asleep! I deliberately moved my face into a frown and took care to keep it on there till I arrived. So I would get the upper hand. I made a lot of racket with my key, but opened up slowly, just getting my frown around the edge of the door—quite timidly, I imagine.

She was sitting up in bed reading by the little bedside lamp. She was about sixty. Her face was smooth and round.

"Hello, I'm Helen Trent" were her words.

I stood there putting my keys away in my bag, for I don't know how long.

I couldn't bear her scrutiny. So I just climbed up onto my bed and fell asleep in my good dress.

Next morning she was moving quietly around when I woke up. While she stood over the sink washing I could see her face in the mirror and the rolls of gray curls around the edge of her faded housecoat. It was as if she'd been torn violently from an old farmhouse but didn't know it yet. I asked her if she was Helen Trent from the radio.

She bobbed her head to show she'd heard and she murmured "No" with a little laugh. She turned around toward me and rubbed her face with a towel. Then she looked right up at me and said, "I'm a widow. I'm going out to Turkey to stay with my son."

I pulled back out of her sight and didn't move again till the door clicked shut behind her. I never could get used to Mrs. Trent or stand her. I don't know why.

When I came up on deck, I saw people clustered at the rail, so I crowded in. Far in the distance I could see a steamship, small but high and blunt at the ends. I was told by a man it was a Russian boat going to Greenland to fish, but I don't know if that makes any sense. He said it reminded him of the Giant Stove at the Chicago World's Fair.

I couldn't take my eyes off that Russian boat. It was gray, and the air was gray and the smoke was black. It was like one of those gauze ensembles Schiaparelli used to put out—always called "Maginot Line" or something. It was certainly a smart combination.

The battle-ax was in her chair next to mine. She was looking right at me, so I couldn't swerve away without producing a lot of trouble. Before I sat down I caught sight of the steward far down the narrow part of the deck, folding up blankets. He nodded to tell me he would bring me my bouillon and biscuits.

I sat down and the battle-ax leaned forward, putting her hard hand on my arm.

"I'm Mrs. Dicky," she said slowly, as if we were having a language lesson. "Mrs. Dicky. I've been waiting to talk to you. I'm traveling alone, and I see that you are, too."

I looked straight ahead and didn't move.

"I'm a widow, and I plan to stay a widow," she murmured. "I had too good a man ever to think of throwing away my memories. My husband, Irwin Dicky, was an industrialist. Inherited a small factory and left me modern industrial plants in three states. Because of something he had in the seat of his pants. If everybody told him no, he'd go ahead and do it. You don't see it nowadays. That man had something."

She went on. "Many's the time I lie in bed and wish I had a man. Oh, yes, I do. You don't have a monopoly on that business. But I would never get married again. And give up my name of Dicky? I'll say I won't. I go in—anywhere—'Here is Mrs. Dicky.' 'The best for Mrs. Dicky!' "

Now I saw the steward coming and I ignored the rest of what she said.

I took the cup and plate onto my lap and thanked him. He was an appealing man named Charles, very alert and humorous.

"Yes, he's a good-looking man," said Mrs. Dicky.

He glanced at her.

"Yes, I mean you, all right. I find lately," she said, turning back toward me, "the serving people only want to do as much as they can get away with, and it's money, money, money. Everybody's like that, these days."

"Yes, I suppose nowadays they'd shoot you for half a quid," said Charles. "Wouldn't they, now?" He looked at her pleasantly. "Wouldn't mean to hurt you!—but he wants the half a quid." He smiled into her blank face. Then she nodded her head just slightly, and he bent down to get her cups and magazines. I watched him walk away with this rubble in his arms. I wanted to get up and go with him, but he wouldn't have known what to do with me, in the midst of his chores.

"Now, just look at that," said Mrs. Dicky, holding up her hand so I could see her ring. "That's costume jewels! But I own the original, too. It's in the A Deck vault. I'm on C Deck, of course. Oh-oh." She shuddered emotionally. "I would be up there myself, but I can't take the noise."

While I was eating my fruit cup at the end of lunch, Jean came along to say hello. She said, "I'll be in my chair," and left. I drank my coffee and went out on deck. The sky was bright. I saw Harry playing shuffleboard, and he waved me over and introduced me to a genial man named Dan. Dan was talking about Roosevelt and the Jews, and how Roosevelt actually was a Jew. While he talked, Harry leaned on his stick and watched his piece to see it didn't slide. Dan made his shot and Harry walked to the line to make his, saying, "What about Teddy, though? *Teddy* Roosevelt was no Jew."

"Well, no, 'course not!" said Dan.

I walked over to my chair. Jean had a pile of *Vogue* magazines beside her and some on her lap.

"I'm throwing away all my clothes. Everything," she said. "I'm going to be strictly *sportif garçonne* now."

"When you get big, you can say you're keeping your golf clubs in there," I said. We stared quietly at her stomach again.

She sighed. "I keep wondering what is wrong with all my belts and Ed has to tell me. He says he had five children during Egyptian times." She took up the magazines. "Oh, let's go back to New York. Listen, 'Tonight: When dusk falls like crumpled black tulle over the city and the belated evening breeze begins to stir, women in penthouses and men in skyscraper offices, debutantes stranded in apartments overlooking the East River, and young gentlemen sated with bond-selling, raise, like a jazz anthem, the question, "Where shall we go tonight?" ' That sounds like Harry. He's a young gentleman sated with bond-selling."

"I just saw Harry over there playing shuffleboard."

"Well, it's so darned similar to polo, you see. Here's the travel guide. Let's see if we're doing all the right things. Oh, what a pity. This happens to be the season for New Hampshire. 'Robert Frost says it is restful just to think of New Hampshire.' And I'm with him. Who is he?"

"Robert Frost, the farmer-poet? Why, he's a poet, and ah . . . a farmer."

"So you know the man's honest. You just know he sits around on barrels and thinks about how to get up the train fare to New York. So he can go to Delmonico's."

Jean turned the pages, murmuring and laughing to herself while I dozed or watched the top of Harry's head, or watched the gray ocean, which of course was surging around us for thousands of miles.

"Oh," said Jean, "don't you want to 'ogle Benchley, Don Stewart, George Kaufman, and other mighty wits, as they hatch the latest quips and cranks' . . . ? And don't you want to ogle them in 'a poured-in halter bodice, with drifting net for the Viennese waltz skirt,' and see Elsa Maxwell, 'dressed in a cowgirl's hat and a sailor's reefer when she gives a dinner at the little bistro at the Port of Antibes'? I'd wear my . . . 'peasant straw cartwheel hat from Nice,' and my perfume: Les Pois de Senteur de Chez Moi by Caron. And that's all I'd wear, because . . ."

"Because Elsa would understand!"

"Yes. Because Elsa would understand. She would understand 'the smell of peas at my house.' "

"What a poetical name," I said, and I actually sighed because the idea of a perfume named for peas reminded me of Hattie.

"Oh, I want to go back," she said after a little silence.

"Don't you want to see Elsa? In her sailor's reefer? Because she's fat, you know. I *think* she's the fat one," I said idly.

"But if we go straight back now we can see Mrs. Eve Symington reenter New York nightlife in a slinky gold dress at the Waldorf. (How do they know what she's going to wear?) Then we can go see *Murder in the Old Red Barn* at the Music Hall. Ha. Here's a play we don't want to miss: 'Their uniforms and their pretty stuffs are an excuse to avoid acting at all. They swagger about, pretty glumly, in magnificent clothes until you wish you were dead.' "

We laughed out loud, and some of the other loungers looked hard at us. The ship was full of cliques.

"That's more like it, anyway," said Jean. "That's why I never dress up."

"Where are you and Ed going, exactly?"

"To Biarritz."

"Isn't that near where Elsa gave her party?"

"I don't think so, dear. Elsa stays on the Riviera. Along with everybody else."

"What's Ed going to do over there?"

"Probably . . . run away when he sees my parents." She closed the magazine and sat back and pushed the curly hair back off her face with two hands. "He'll run away when he sees Mother on the dock, tugging on her 'strength-through-joy' girdle. Then my father will put on his golf shoes and run after him."

"Well, why are you even going?"

"Oh, I don't know. It'll be all right. They'll go have a drink man to man and get plastered. And then my father will tell

Ed a lot of sex jokes and call him 'son.' Mother and I will be at home getting all nervous. Then they'll come in and ignore us completely. But that's what I want. See, with Ed, every-thing's always at white heat."

Then we watched the Bolshie coming toward us with the doctor. They were not speaking and they were in a hurry. To me, this was an absorbing sight. As they came up, I saw that the doctor was in front; probably he was trying to get away.

The Bolshie used her shoulders to pull the rest of her body along, and these rose and fell on either side of her head, which looked like a ball because her hair was so short. Jean called, "Hel-lo, you two!" in a gay voice, as if the two of them were lovers, and she had introduced them. The doctor nodded quickly, as if trying to hide his unhappiness, and they both kept going, the Bolshie not even turning. Strangely enough, she had dropped her hankie on the deck. Jean said, "Well, if *that's* not the oldest trick in the book."

"You're just *like* Ed, though," I told Jean.

"Do you think so? He's much fairer-skinned. You know, when he was a baby, his mother used to rub Vaseline all over his body, and one day he slipped right out of her hands! She didn't even realize it, because she was chatting with her friends, and he was just crawling around on the boardwalk. He says that was the day he decided to run away for good."

I began to daydream about my mother, and how she would almost burst out crying if I cut my finger. And then I dozed off after staring up at the clouds. Jean asked me whether I was sleeping.

"I wanted to ask you, what's it like having a job? Is it a lot of fun being on your own like that? Coming home and making your own little dinner? I think it would be grand. I love department stores, anyway. I go to a dressmaker, because it's supposed to be cheaper than the ready-made. I have an old lady I go to in New York. She actually made my first dress—which she still remembers. And when I was about thirteen years old, I'd say, 'Can't you make this a little tighter? You know. For when I'm older?' And she'd say, 'Oh, yes, if you say so,' and she'd pin it all up to perfection. And, then, the minute I'd walk out the door, she'd run to the phone and tell my mother. But if you go to a store, you can spend the whole day trying on things . . . like, waitress uniforms, evening gowns . . ."

I thought of how very happy this would make Mr. Lazarus, who tried to make his store as much like a circus as possible, and I told Jean so.

"He sounds swell. Who is he?" she said.

"He owns Lazarus's."

"Does he?" said Jean. "That reminds me of all those movies where the beautiful girl—beautiful but bad—is just there lying in the gutter, and then she sees man's shoes standing beside her face. She looks up and it's Ray Milland! And Ray Milland is wearing a beautiful suit, and he has his little lips tucked in, and he says 'Get up, honey.' And she gets up, and they go in a taxi to the nearest department store, and he buys her beautiful clothes—whatever she desires—right down to the underwear. Don't laugh! Because she still knows that, deep down, she's a bad girl, and that's how it ends. Back in the gutter, in her old cotton dress and soiled gloves."

"I'll bet that's where the doctor and the Bolshie girl were going."

"Where?" said Jean.

"Well, there's a tobacconist on board."

"Yes, she probably was lying somewhere face down, and he came along and said, 'Get up, Bolshie, darling, and I'll get you some cigars.' "

"I'm a servant of mankind, Bolshie. You can believe in me."

"And she bursts out crying and says, 'I never thought a Bolshie like me could ever hook a doctor like you, sir.'

"Let's go look for them, how 'bout it?" said Jean. "I'm tired of sitting down. And then we'll get something to drink. Some of those 'dear little iced things.' "

We threw back our blankets and stood up.

"Don't just leave your blanket, Jean," I said. "Fold it, otherwise Charles has to do it."

"Oh, darling, *please* don't fall for Charles," said Jean suddenly. "We're going to find you somebody rich. Ed's already thinking about it."

"I didn't fall for Charles."

"Don't you like Harry at all?"

"No, not at all," I said, surprised. "He's not my type, even remotely," I went on.

"Well, who is your type?" she said as we walked along.

"I don't know. Charles, I guess."

"Because he works with his two hands? You're so silly, because that's nothing. Harry *adores* you, and I'm his confidante."

"Do *you* like Harry? He's so weak," I told her.

"Oh, no, I don't especially, since you mention it. He looks nice from a distance, though. He's got that *je ne sais quoi*."

It was breezy and the sun was starting to go down. We swerved around two girls playing deck tennis and squealing because the wind was carrying the birdie around in all directions. We forgot to look for the little romantic couple we had been interested in and went right into the bar. It was already busy in there.

They were all talking about their costumes for the costume

39

party that was supposed to be the next night—our last night before docking in Cherbourg, where I was getting off. A woman was leaning way over the bar and asking the steward if he wore a nightcap, and if she could borrow it.

"You've been on this ship four days and four nights and you don't know yet if Cyril here—the suavest fellow on board—wears a nightcap?" asked the red-faced man beside her. "Denice!"

"Shh! Oh, don't," said the woman. She looked angrily around at all of us.

"Well, don't ask me because I certainly don't know," he continued. "Cyril's never asked *me* to join him in his hammock. Not yet, anyway," and he winked at the steward, who was working away, smiling but not looking up.

"I'll have bourbon and ginger, and my friend wants a gin fizz," I told Cyril.

"Perhaps *you* know," said the man to me.

"Know what?"

"Why, about Cyril. How he sleeps at night. Whether he wears a nightcap, or whether he doesn't, for example. Or whether he wears his socks to bed."

Wanting to side with Cyril, I said, "He doesn't wear socks to bed and he doesn't use a nightcap."

"Well, well!" shouted the man through the outburst of laughing that followed. "What are you? About sixteen?"

At this moment Cyril put the drinks in my hands and Jean and I walked out.

"The swine," said Jean as we walked back toward the stern, our eyes on the sunset that was flaring up against half the sky. "It's good luck Charles wasn't there to hear it."

I told her I was only glad Ed wasn't there, and I asked her not to tell him about it.

"I won't, unless he begs me," she said in a kind voice.

"I don't like him thinking about finding me a husband either."

"I know it," said Jean. "He's horrible."

There were quite a few people around watching the sky. It really did look like sheets of red satin, as all the women were saying. To think that it was all done for no one in particular—that it was just done every night or so, ship or no ship. I found that after all I was happier turning my back on it. Jean had already turned around, and so we stood side by side with our drinks in our hands and our elbows on the rail. Straight ahead across the expanse of deck were the glass doors and the bar beyond them, where they were probably still teasing Cyril and pointing out at me. Above that and some way forward was the A Deck. The A Deck people were crowding around to see the sunset, too. At times during the voyage I had noticed they just stood there and looked down at us, which caused us Second Class people to get mad, as if they thought we were their peasants. However, nobody wanted to appear to notice them, so they played only a small role in our lives.

Jean touched my arm. "She's waving at us," she said, pointing.

There was a small, neat woman at the rail, and she did seem to be waving at us. She was wearing white slacks, and she had dark hair pinned up wide at the sides, and big black beads tight around her neck. Since we just stared at her, she stopped waving. At this moment Mrs. Dicky came up.

"Did you keep an eye on my chair for me?" she asked me.

Jean said, "I know what it is. That must be Wallis Simpson! She's always trying to get to know me better. Wally!"

This was just when Wally Simpson was the most famous woman in the world, so this was very amusing to us. Jean and I waved and laughed loudly, and quite soon the woman turned away.

"Who's that? Who's that?" said Mrs. Dicky excitedly.

"It's Wally Simpson!" said Jean. "She wants to be friends with us!"

"Oh! Oh!" exclaimed the battle-ax, hurriedly raising her purse and waving it.

Now the woman walked away, but several men and women still standing there waved back.

"I don't understand," said Mrs. Dicky. "Was that Wallis?"

"Oh, doesn't she dress beautifully?" said Jean. "She looked so *sportif*!"

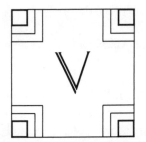

IT SEEMED to me from then on that the stewards were all friendly to me, and I began to feel the story of what I had said in the bar was getting around. A woman at the next table from mine at dinner that night spilled her spoonful of soup on the dining steward's sleeve when he reached for something, and even while he was setting that right, he was glancing up at me. But maybe he just pitied me because I had come into the dining room with my hair wet. It certainly was an unusual thing to do, but I had had to wash it in the afternoon instead of at bedtime, to avoid Mrs. Trent.

I ate my chicken croquettes as fast as I could, with my eyes fixed on the frilly lampshade, and walked out right after dessert. I had brought a Fannie Hurst book from my cabin, and I was going to try to read it. At that time of my life, I had only really read two books—Mrs. *Wiggs of the Cabbage Patch* and *Evangeline*—and I thought all books must be like either one or the other. I went to a corner of the library, which was a paneled room with wing chairs in groups and low lamps on little tables. I felt from the first page that this book, *Appas-sionata*, was more an *Evangeline* type of book, but I couldn't grasp it. It wasn't told in first person or third person, but in second person. It was like this:

> To yawn as Laura yawned made you shimmer of the ecstasy of the flesh.

Laura was a Catholic girl who was engaged to be married. Her mother and older sister were flabby from too much child-bearing. It said her father looked like a chimpanzee.

> You knew! There was something in Father's squattiness, of a low powerfully built chimpanzee!

I was lonesome and wanted to get nearer Hattie, but I couldn't stand it and put the book away. In those days I was always so afraid of being imposed on.

I looked around the vast room and saw that Ed was there, writing at one of the desks. He soon got up and came over to me, and I asked him where he'd been all day.

"I've been wiring Russia, Louise. Trying to get over there for a visit. I just want to drift down the Volga and see all the people working."

I thought this must mean he was leaving Jean.

He dragged a chair up to mine and sat down and pulled out a cigarette. "See, I'm going to go over there and look around, make up a few slogans, and come back and throw together a little book. And don't *tell* me it's already been done! What are you doing in here like a hermit?"

I couldn't answer. I could only stare at him.

"What's the matter?"

"You don't mean to say you're leaving Jean!"

Now he stared, his cigarette at arm's length, as if he was desperate to see me clearly. "You mystify me, girl."

"Well, if you go over to Russia . . ."

"Oh!" He laughed, sitting back. "That's just a job. I'd never leave Jean, not even if she asked me to. And you can tell her I said so."

"I'm so glad."

He peered at me. "Quaint little thing, aren't you? What are you reading there?" He grabbed the book off the table and turned it over in a way that seemed to ridicule it, then opened it up and read a little bit—silently, to my relief. Then he started to laugh and read out, " 'To yawn as Laura could yawn, was to be as complete as a full moon.' Pardon me, but what does that mean?" He sighed and put it back. Then he was silent for a while, just smoking. I began to notice low talking from the middle of the room, probably from a high-backed davenport that faced the other way. I felt homesick and I took Hattie's book onto my lap.

Ed put out his cigarette and rubbed his face with both hands. When he took them away his cheeks were redder than ever and his hair stood up in all directions.

"So how's Cyril?" he said. "Ha! You little vixen. Well, it's an ugly business, and you know," he said, putting his hand on my knee, "it's breaking Harry's heart."

"Oh, stop it, Ed. You shouldn't be so stupid!"

He looked at me, grimacing. "It must be the Fannie Hurst. She's poison to women," he said wearily. "Come on and I'll find you something good to read. Something with some testicles."

He stood up, and to make amends I went with him along the bookcase that lined the wall. He made me sit in the big davenport and then turned to search the shelves.

The people I had heard but not seen turned out to be Mrs.

Trent and the Servant of Mankind! Mrs. Trent was saying, "And I remember another time, I was on the porch one evening in a rainstorm. It was too dark to read, but it wasn't too dark to knit. My husband came home and he said for me to get ready my things for a train ride. Well, we had to go to West Virginia. There was a coal strike. Bituminous. We were on the train at dawn, going through Kentucky. And when we got in West Virginia the children would be at the station hooting at the train, and a bad tomato was thrown at my husband, and it ran down the screen." We all nodded. The doctor said to Mrs. Trent, "Of course I am frequently called up to the bridge."

"The captain, you mean? You have to go and talk to the captain?" said Mrs. Trent.

"Oh, yes," said the doctor. "Sometimes he just wants to talk things over with me. Well, as I say, please feel free to come to me with any little problem—professional or nonprofessional, of course!" At this he winked at me.

"Well, thank you," said Mrs. Trent quietly. "You know, I appreciate that very much. It does feel so alone on this big ship sometimes."

After he had gone, Mrs. Trent and I sat there perfectly still on the large davenport, with her last words sort of hovering around us in the air, it seemed to me, and coming down to slap me in the face very lightly, like moths.

"Here, girlie," said Ed as he turned and dropped a little book, which I caught in my hands. "*The Rock Pool.* It's got balls and it's by a guy named Cyril. So! How do you do?" he added to Mrs. Trent. "This girl here doesn't have anything to read and it's made her cross."

Mrs. Trent sympathized, probably forgetting whom he was talking about. I stood up, not wanting to get trapped with her. She looked up at us in a troubled way.

"You know, I heard today that we might be forced to stop at the Azores tomorrow. Do you think so?"

"Why would we do that?" said Ed, sitting down beside her on the other side and bending toward her as if she were mentally ill.

"Well, you see, they're islands, and I understood from the doctor that they may be running out of food. Apparently our captain always passes close to them and looks for a distress signal."

"Oh, that's good," said Ed. He sat back with an air of really settling down. I couldn't pummel him and then drag him away—I was too disheartened to go farther than the chair opposite, where I sat and pretended to read. Above my book I watched Ed, all wound up and attentive, staring at Mrs. Trent's profile, while she gazed like a sibyl straight ahead, probably going over past wheat harvests in her mind.

"Are you traveling for pleasure?" inquired Ed sincerely.

"It does seem that everything is going sour in the world," said Mrs. Trent slowly. "I've felt that way ever since way back when the Depression started."

"Oh, I *know* it," said Ed encouragingly.

"My son had gone down to the store to hear the radio after school let out in the afternoon. Well, he ran back as fast as he could, and told me the stock market had crashed! He looked so frightened, I believe he thought it was some kind of a truck. . . . And I remember they were all saying this must be the rending of the earth for the Day of Judgment. But I said no. And now there's going to be another war."

"Oh, buck up, Mrs. Trent," said Ed.

Later he said to me, "Mrs. Trent's a real hellcat." But I couldn't joke about her. She was an object of dread to me, and she never harmed me, so I can't explain it. I said good night to Ed, and went out on deck and peered down at the

ghostly wake. The sea was more luminous than the sky, because the moon was hidden by clouds. It was a mysterious
night, with nothing happy or romantic about it, and the
thrashing of the water sounded so dreary. It agitated me to
think that the engines had run continually during every second
of the voyage so far, which that night seemed to me to go
back fifteen years. Why couldn't they turn them off for an
hour, and let all the passengers and crew come out on deck
and stroke the railings or hose the sides or something? But
that's something interesting about sea travel; I think that if
the engines were stopped in mid-ocean, even if it was done
on purpose, all the passengers would start screaming at that
moment.

I imagine I was tired of being idle so long and I felt tired
of everybody joking all the time. Standing there, I thought I
was really tired for good—that I should really be two days out
of New York and not two days out of Cherbourg with all my
work left to do. But of course it doesn't happen that way when
you're nineteen years old. For example, the next night I won
a dance contest.

Pretty soon a man in ship's uniform came and stood nearby,
also looking down at the water.

"It's cold down there," he said humorously.

"I suppose so," I said.

"Well, don't jump then."

"I won't."

"Why should you when you've still got books to read?"

I laughed at him and tried to look him over in the dim
light.

"I'm Wentworth, staff captain," he said politely. "Very nice
to meet you. Hm. What are you reading?"

I looked down at my books, and he stepped up and took

them from me. He said, "Ah," as he looked them over, and then he handed them back. "Very nice. May I escort you indoors? It's getting cold, don't you think?"

I was looking at the sky, trying to think of an answer. The clouds had broken up and were rushing ahead of us in hordes. I felt my encounter with Mrs. Trent had robbed me of my happiness for all time.

"Too much grandeur isn't good for young ladies."

"Is that so?" I said rudely, yet not knowing how to follow it up.

"That's so. They run the risk of turning into mystics and then they, ah, won't wear their pretty clothes anymore."

He was relaxed, whether I was nice to him or not. He just chuckled and put his hand under my elbow and we went in. I went, because he was an elderly man. We walked in and sat down at the bar, which was deserted, except that Cyril came running when Wentworth called his name.

Wentworth had a reddish face, with distinguished bags under his eyes, and he was quite tall and handsome for an older man.

"And so, miss," he said after giving directions to Cyril. "Let's drink and forget our troubles, shall we?"

"Why? Did you think I was going to jump in?" I said without gratitude.

"I told you. I just hate to see a girl turn mystic."

"Well, I'm not the type," I told him, "so it was never a possibility."

Cyril set out little cups of coffee, which Wentworth ignored.

"Oh, no?" he said, squinting at me and tilting his head. "I'm not so sure. You'll grant me you're absentminded, and . . . wistful."

"Oh, no, I'm not."

"She's a lovely and kind young woman," said Cyril, who was leaning back against the sink with his arms folded.

"Oh, go to blazes, why don't you?" said Wentworth to Cyril. "These stupid young fellows," he said to me, "are always getting in my way. Yes, I suppose I'm at the bottom of a twelve-page list, with all my own stewards ahead of me. I can see it. Way at the bottom, 'Old Wentworth,' or 'Poor Old Wentworth.' Oh, don't tell me!"

All this was making me giddy. I laughed wildly. For a few seconds he pretended to be scared. Then he narrowed his eyes. "I don't know what you're laughing about," he said. "Is it so funny to break an old man's heart? Do you think so, Cyril?"

"No, I don't, sir. It's sad."

"You see?" said Wentworth to me. "Cyril's sorry for me. Are you taking a laugh cure, then?"

He gave me his handkerchief and I covered my face with it. Then I pulled it down to just below my eyes and I said, "If you're so discouraged, why don't you go and play canasta with some of the older ladies? They may like you."

"Oh, thank you! Cyril! Did you hear that?" he said, still watching me. " 'Sod off!' she tells me. 'Leave Cyril and me alone.' "

"Oh, they all want that. They know I'm fond of them," said Cyril.

"Just look at the prancing baboon!" exclaimed Wentworth. Then, with an air of getting serious, he said to me, "Is this true?"

"No, we don't care for Cyril either," I said.

"Ha! I'm sticking around then. And this girl wants another drink, steward. And make it hotter this time. Put the whiskey in the coffee before you blow it out that thing, can't you? My, my," he said, facing me again, "so this is romance. My

God, I'm glad you picked me! You aren't leaving the ship at Cherbourg, are you?"

"Azores."

He nodded with his eyes wide and chuckled.

"Because they may need food."

"That's so. Never thought of it till this moment. Why don't you go get your things ready, then, and meet me on deck around—let's see—three o'clock, and I'll help you up over the rail."

"I changed my mind."

"Well, if you're sure," he said, and looked down at his watch. "Now, miss, I'm wanted somewhere in five minutes. But I would not dream of leaving you here alone with Cyril, so, may I walk you to your cabin?"

I got down off my stool and took his arm. He steered me back around to the bar, where my books were sitting. I saluted Cyril and said, "Good night, Cyril," and Wentworth said, "Good night, Cyril," and after making a complete revolution, we went through the double door side by side, then in single file went down a staircase, Wentworth patting my shoulder and saying, "Steady on."

Side by side again, I held his arm right to me. It wasn't like me, of course, but I did it. It is as vivid to me as yesterday afternoon; unbearably vivid, too, when I consider that Wentworth has most certainly left this earth by now. What is there now, in these times, to compensate for that, and all the other things and people that made those days? Rhinestone cowboys? What does that mean? Though I live in it, I feel that only fools believe that this is still the world! I catch myself thinking this way.

We marched along quickly, while I said to him things like "I'm sure you're not too old for love," and he'd say, "Who said I was?"

I took hold of a red fire ladder on the wall and pretended I couldn't move. I said, "We'll go to the Azores!"

He looked at something over my head, with a bored expression.

"We'll lash ourselves to crates of food and float. You must know the currents!"

"And what do we do when the natives come down to the beach and push us off with poles?"

"Oh, we'll make it! You and I will build a hut for the sake of total romance."

"And when you tire of me, you'll let me stay on as your great-grandfather?"

"Maybe I will."

"Thank you!" he'd say, and he would urge me along.

"I'll push you around the Azores in a wheelchair."

"That's kind," he murmured.

A cabin door behind us opened but did not shut. We were making a lot of racket. We continued in whispers to the door of my cabin—whispers that were also loud. While I searched for my key, he whispered to me, "Who's in there with you?" I put my mouth up to his ear to tell him but ended by kissing his ear. I didn't want to bring Mrs. Trent into this beautiful situation. I was in an uncanny mood. As he kept absolutely still, I kept on kissing his ear. I kissed every part of it for a long while, feeling quite at home. Then he whispered, "I said, who's in there?"

Now we really laughed like fiends. Somehow during this he opened the door and I found myself in the dark with Mrs. Trent's breathing for company.

I felt such deep regret. I supposed Wentworth was married or a strong philosophical bachelor—too big to care for a girl like me, though he wouldn't mind helping out and acting comradely. Again and again I reviewed what I had done, while Mrs. Trent's breaths came up to me like the sound of an irritating pounding drum. I woke up next morning reckless and unhappy, because I thought I had lost my chance to be in love.

WHILE I ate my breakfast I saw Harry lounging and smoking in the doorway. Then he disappeared, but when I
walked through he jumped out of somewhere and said, "Oh,
hello. Care to take a stroll?" Though he spoke so casually,
his hand was shaking. Actually, he trembled all the time, but
I didn't know. Anyway, I agreed. Maybe I was actually trying
to be nice to somebody!

We descended the wide staircase that was like a carnival
ride. On the walls were pictures of Europeans landing in the
New World with Indians peering out at them from behind
bushes. We came out in the elegant hallway where the shops
were, and side by side without talking we walked along, staring
stupidly into them. Then I said, "Did you want to say something to me?" and I glared at him.

He blushed and suddenly went into the tobacconist's. I went
back and started up the stairs, wondering whether I might see
Wentworth sometime that day. Then Harry came pounding

up behind me. He held out his cigarette pack as he came up alongside and said, "I just had to get some of these."

Then at the top he blocked my way and said, "I guess I was pretty loathsome the other night, so, I'm sorry. It's just that you're so damned attractive."

"I don't care about it, I don't mind," I said. "I'm going out on deck." I was trying not to sound mean, but I thought the situation was over. I had no idea he'd follow me out. But he was in good spirits now, having debased himself.

When we stepped through the door, he steered me around to the right—away from where Jean and Ed might be sitting. I went impersonally to the rail, and he told me about going drinking and slumming in Harlem just before the ship sailed.

"Where are you from, anyway?" he asked. "Ed said you were a Mennonite, but of course I didn't believe him."

"New York."

"Really? I'm from Chicago. But I know plenty of New York people, like these people I was just telling you about—Bill Spalding and his wife—well, they're actually from North Carolina. So, how do you like the working girl life? Get to meet all kinds of people? Plenty of low people?" He raised his cigarette to his lips and his hand was trembling. Then I heard the sound of Ed's laugh somewhere behind us. I said, "Oh, I have to speak to Ed!"

Without knowing exactly where he was, I just walked blindly off toward the sound, and did find him swatting at the air with his shuffleboard stick while Dan played. He watched me approach and probably saw Harry behind me. When I reached him I realized Harry was still behind me, so since I couldn't say what I'd meant to say, I just stared.

After a moment he put out his hand and said, "I guess you don't know me. Red Mike, Socialist."

Harry snorted. Then Ed went to play his turn and I went with him, leaving Harry to stand there.

"You've met," said Ed, gesturing toward Dan. "Dan's a Socialist, too."

"He's telling lies again," said Dan to me in a humorous voice. "Why there's a Brooks Brothers label on every suit he owns. And on every suit I own!" he added, laughing.

"But I gave *away* my suits, Dan."

"Oh, yeah? To whom?"

"To a convent. In the garment district," said Ed. "They make them into holy objects for the poor."

"Oh, sure!"

"Well, Dan, you wouldn't know this, but poor people like to have little pieces of cloth around. Especially if a nun has touched them."

"Don't he beat all?" said Dan in disbelief. "He'd sit and lie all day if somebody'd listen to him."

Ed always assumed a shrugging sort of manner when he was making up lies, and so now he asked me if I cared to go along and hear Dan and him talk up socialism in the bar. I told him it was too early for me, and he said, "It's never too early to talk up socialism."

"Come on, honey," said Dan, taking my arm. "We'll find you something without anything harmful in it. I know how little girls are. Lord, that Ed's as crazy as a loon. But he's a *funny* damn guy and I enjoy anybody who can make me laugh."

The Bolshie was sitting alone at the bar when we got there, sort of leaning forward on one arm. The steward behind the bar—it was not Cyril—stood awkwardly staring the other way, but smiled happily when we came in. I declined the drinks Dan described to me and turned around to rest my elbows on the bar and looked out. The same two silly girls were playing deck tennis again. I thought I might like to try it after lunch.

Dan leaned over and confidentially asked me who the Bolshie was. "I'm sorry," he said laughing, "but I'm damned if she ain't the image of Senator Bilbo."

"No need to whisper!" said Ed. "He's the handsomest guy in the Senate."

"If you like 'em that way," said Dan. "But what's she so down about?" He tapped my arm. "What ails that girl?"

"She wants a drink and can't get one," I said in the callous way we all talked about her.

Dan couldn't get over it. After a pause he said, "I don't believe I ever saw a woman looking so mean."

The Bolshie sighed loudly as if she were on a stage, and dragged herself down off her stool and went out. The steward didn't even look her way. She was everything we all didn't want to be.

When it was just us three again, Dan's spirits seemed to rise, and he told us a long story about himself and a trio of "sporting girls." I thought he meant these girls were good sports. He and Ed laughed themselves sick—not just at the end but all through it. Ed would throw his head back out of sight, and when he sat up again it would be dark like a spiced apple and his eyes would be all puffy. Dan merely opened his mouth when he was overcome, and kept it open in the shape of a box, while he went HA, HA, HA. I'm not sure I remember it all. I don't even know if it's all that funny. This is the story: The year before, in Philadelphia, Dan had met three sporting girls. They were in a bar when they decided to go out and get some dinner. They were feeling no pain. Leaving the place, Dan had wandered into the spotlight around a girl singing, and finding himself there, he had mimicked her for a couple of minutes. Then, while the four of them were waiting outside for a taxi, a man came out and told Dan to go back inside. Dan was startled and thought he recognized the man as "some big juju man in Philadelphia." He decided right then, this man probably owned the bar, and that the singer was his girlfriend, and that now he and his goons were going to teach him a lesson. He was scared, and the girls were all screaming and jumping for a cab. Suddenly one drove up. Dan said to the man, "Why, you big pimp!" and made a fist. The girls opened the door of the cab and Dan dove into it, the man raving at him from the sidewalk. Next thing, the girls were in beside him, shouting at the driver to go faster, and the driver drove right into the side of another car just pulling away from the curb. Not fifty feet away from where the juju man was standing. I remember Dan shaking his head and wiping his eyes and saying, "Now a thing like that can't happen!"

Then the juju man ran back inside. Then another fellow came out and said he had just wanted Dan to get a favor from his congressman—a liquor license or something.

"I've been back to Philly," Dan said, "but I never looked up those girls. Two of 'em were sisters. At least I think that's what they said. Well, Dora keeps me reined in pretty good. The fact is, I married too young. I can appreciate Dora, Ed, I can appreciate her. What's your girl's name, Ed?"

"Jean."

"Hm," said Dan. Then he crept his hand along the bar toward where my arm was. He told me I was a funny little thing, but that he was nothing but an old fool.

I smiled. Out of the blue Ed said, "You know, Dan, you should try to resist temptation. Make 'Service' your motto."

"He's right, you know, I should," said Dan cozily to me.

I had never been near a man like Dan. He wore a diamond ring and he had lotion on his hair. When I asked him what he did, he looked hurt. "Oh, let's not talk about that, honey!" he said to me.

He was one of those men who think girls live to hear mushy

words around the clock. I thought he was fascinating, though. I didn't see how someone so undignified could be a success in life. Most likely he couldn't have explained it to me. He was just an innocent. Ed told me that Dan had never had a conscious thought in his life, and had told him so.

Dan told another good story at some point that day, of which I can remember only the ending. A little guy is holding the coats and saying, "C'mon, let's you guys fight!"

I announced that I knew a good story, and had them staring into my face with expectant looks—Ed particularly, when I said it was about an old Rough Rider. Then I remembered where the story came from and I told them to never mind the story because I'd forgotten it. They both looked so disappointed. Ed said, "If only she could remember what the fellow said to the old Rough Rider!"

"I love to hear a woman tell a story like a man," said Dan gazing at me. "I just love it."

"What was it the fellow said?" Ed asked me. "Can't you recall it? Wasn't it, 'Bet you're an old Rough Rider'?"

Dan urged me to have a drink to help me remember. I accepted, and he said to Ed, "She's not so high and mighty!" That made Ed laugh.

We heard the noon whistle, and Dan had to rush away to the smoking room for the daily pools. One single woman had won it the past two days, but Dan was sure it wasn't rigged. You couldn't rig a thing like that, he told us.

Ed and I strolled along to our chairs to pass the time till luncheon, and there was Jean dozing, with Mrs. Dicky looking over my chair at her, and tapping her wrist so that her bracelet banged against the chair arm.

"Well, here you are!" she said to us. "Did you have a drink at this hour?"

"Yes, Mrs. Dicky," said Ed solemnly.

We seated ourselves and she leaned toward me.

"You've got expensive clothes! How's that?"

I should have said, "Men give them to me!" But I just pretended I hadn't heard her and that I was asleep already.

Soon she got up and went away. We called her the It Girl now. Ed started it after she had taken him aside and told him the urges she still had at night.

When she was gone Jean came to life, sitting up and pinching Ed's cheek. "I was dreaming! Not right then—I was awake—but before the whistle. Can't remember it, though. But all of us were there, everybody on the whole ship, and the baby was a great big tall boy, college age at least! He and I walked everywhere hand in hand. He was like our little *attendant*, sort of!"

Ed laughed at her, and Jean squirmed around in her seat and threw off the blanket. "I've had to sit here with the It Girl meanwhile. I didn't move, but she knew I was awake, and she was talking about you two under her breath to get a rise out of me." She imitated Mrs. Dicky's voice and her insinuating speech. "They're in the bar now, side by side."

"Actually, it's her I love," said Ed, tapping out a cigarette. "Can you blame me?"

I was amazed at the vileness of the It Girl. I took a cigarette from Ed and I told them Mrs. Dicky was "a dirty go-by-ground," old words from my grandmother that I had never used. That made them howl. Ed came over and kissed my cheek, saying to Jean, "Look how pretty she is!" I said, "No, I'm mad."

The girls who played deck tennis from morning till night went past, slowing down and saying "Oh, hello" to Ed. Then they pounced on the steward. They wanted a special net, a Blinko net. It's opaque and goes right down to the ground, so that you don't know what's happening until the little thing comes and hits you on the head. He told them it was almost time for luncheon. The girls groaned. Jean, Ed and I all stood up.

Jean stared out to sea and murmured that she wished she had some shampoo, so she could wash her hair and not have to go eat lunch. I said she could come and use mine, and I'd join her.

And that's what we did. We were just idling along the middle deck toward the stairs that led to my cabin, Jean trying to recall the name of the biscuit manufacturing company that Ed's grandfather had started, then backed out of just before it got tremendously rich during the Roaring Twenties. I happened to look through one of those crisscross hatches in the floor and miraculously saw my friend Wentworth standing down there. I also recognized his voice saying, "Oh, to be sure not," and laughing.

I was excited and happy to see him again. I took Jean's arm in mine and led her down the stairs in a hurry while she went on muttering syllables—because the biscuits had a funny name that she was anxious for me to hear. We went down some stairs, and soon we were really dashing down the companion-way I believed Wentworth was at the end of. Jean thought we were rushing to my cabin. Both Jean and I were dressed all in white as it happened, and when we finally rushed up to Wentworth—who was leaning in the doorway of a broom closet—he looked up and said, "Girl tennis champions!" Then he threw up his hands as if in fear and said, "We don't play!"

"That's what *you* say!" said Jean gaily, though she didn't know who he was.

"Come over here, please," I said secretively to him, tossing my head in a direction away from the broom closet.

His eyes opened up a little bit, and he murmured, "Just a minute" to someone inside the closet, and the three of us moved down the hallway. There we stood in a confidential

circle, both Jean and Wentworth inclining their heads courteously toward mine and fixing their eyes on nothing, while I looked at the gold threads of Wentworth's little badges. Then suddenly I was scared out of my wits. I really didn't recognize myself in this setting. So then, stiffly, I said, "Well, I just wanted to thank you for a nice time last night."

"The pleasure was mine," said Wentworth with a tiny bow.

"What did you do?" said Jean.

"Well," Wentworth began, "she came along, and made me go sit in a bar with her. She made me drink—liquor drinks—"

"And when you woke up your front teeth were missing?" said Jean.

"Yes! Of course they were missing. She's a frightfully powerful girl. Really almost a giantess."

I pulled my arm out from Jean's and went rushing back down the hall the way we had come. I thought they were joking to cover their shame at my behavior, which I felt had been insane.

I hurried to my doorway down at the other end and went in, in the hope that Jean would start back up the stairs alone and I could signal to her. I stood inside with the door open a tiny bit, waiting, and was embarrassed to see Wentworth come into view around the bottom of the stairs, Jean beside him. Of course he knew where my cabin was, and I soon realized they were both looking—not in my direction—but right at me. He patted her shoulder and went back out of sight toward the broom closet, and she came down the hall. I stepped back to let her in, then went into the bathroom as if it were urgent that I get the shampoo.

"You didn't have to run away," she said. "Did you want him to come after you instead of me? I wasn't sure."

Of course I couldn't answer. I was staring in horror at myself in the mirror.

"He wanted to tell you he'll get you whatever you need for your costume."

I still couldn't reply. I was such a ninny, and it wasn't just pride, it was ignorance, too. As if I were the first human being on earth to get a crush on a man. Jean sat hunched over on the lower bunk and began carrying on a conversation by herself—out of kindness to me.

"I want us to go as Kate Smith and Helen Traubel," she said. "All the women are going as Wallis. It's *not* exactly original. I wouldn't be caught dead going as Wallis! She's no better than she should be."

"That Wallis. I know it," I said, timidly coming out.

Jean went into the shower first—still chattering—while I lay in my bed, and when I came out from washing my hair, she was up there in her camisole and man's underpants looking at a magazine.

"I used plenty of Mrs. Trent's Quelques Fleurs powder, and now I'm reading her *National Geographic*," she said without looking up.

I toweled my hair in front of the mirror and then climbed up next to her and stretched out. You had to stretch out because the ceiling was so low. There was a small rotary fan on the lamp and I turned it on. Together we looked at the magazine, which Jean had perched on her stomach.

"This is handy, isn't it?" she said.

"Yes," I said boldly, looking at her stomach. "Well, you really just look a tiny bit fat."

She laughed. She started fussing with her hair. "I don't like to crush my 'bob,' lying on it when it's soaking wet." She leaned out over the edge to look around the cabin. "Want to sit side by side on the dresser? Or, I've got a good idea! Why don't we go to the beauty parlor and get it set? It's going to look pretty loathsome otherwise."

I pondered this.

"Why not, anyway?" she went on. "We aren't savages! And, then, tomorrow when we're getting off, it will give us so much courage."

"I don't need any courage."

"Of course you do!"

"I know I do." Then I said, "I'm going to need courage if I'm going to see Wentworth again."

"Gosh, he's attractive," said Jean. "I really like him. I'm sure he's in love with you."

"It isn't true."

"If you'd only seen how he looked at you."

"He looked at me just the way you look at a puppy when it starts whining and you can't tell what's wrong with it," and as I said this I was trying to take the magazine into my own hands.

Jean propped herself up on her elbow. "You're bereft of your senses. Don't you know anything? . . . You're only sixteen years old at the most, anyway," she went on in a lighthearted voice.

"I'm nineteen."

"Well, I'm twenty, I'm married, and that explains the difference. And I promise you, that man out there regards you as a poignant flower he can't touch with his vile old hands. Not that I think he's vile or anything," she added.

I kept my eyes on the bows I was tying in the sash of my robe. Jean herself was becoming an object of fascination to me, the careless way she tossed these opinions around so that they seemed like facts. How did she know it all? How could

Wentworth be vile? As for myself, I knew I was retail to my finger ends and a hard worker; any person less flowerlike couldn't be imagined. So her whole explanation was lost on me.

"Well," said Jean, "he didn't try to kiss you or anything, did he?"

"No."

"But he was really kind to you, wasn't he?"

"Just helping a passenger!"

She laughed in my face, making it seem like the kindest praise possible.

"Let's just look at the magazine," I said.

"We'll look at the Egyptian objects. See? Aren't they pretty? Cockroach pins." She put the magazine down. "Then when our hair is dry, we'll go up to the salon and we'll get our hair set. We can get finger waves. Or a nice marcel. That will help our costumes, anyway."

"Who are we going as again?"

"Helen Traubel and Kate Smith. That's what I was thinking."

"Would that be funny?"

"Yes."

"Is Ed going as something?"

"Oh, I don't know. He might think up something sick at the last minute. He's still down there sending telegrams to Amtorg—Russia, you know."

"I couldn't tell if he was serious."

"He'll be serious as long as they don't want him. If all of a sudden they invited him, he'd lose interest. Forget all about it."

"Jean, do you ever call him Eddie?"

"No. Do you want me to?"

"Do you think he'd mind if I did?"

"Don't you know that he loves attention of any kind?"

"I'd like to call him Eddie because Ed sounds like a thug's name. It doesn't seem to suit him."

"Well, don't tell him that. It would hurt him."

I always associate this conversation, which was a diversionary tactic on my part, with the sight of Jean's translucent hands, with the bright red polish on her oval nails, holding up the magazine. I wonder how she managed during the war in Biarritz. I hope Ed wasn't fool enough to leave her there.

"His mother calls him 'Ed-weird' or something," she went on. "She's descended from the Germanic tribes."

We passed the time until our hair was dry examining pictures of objects from ancient Egypt. The way they used gold and precious gems made us indignant—which was actually just a form of high spirits. For example, there was a lapis lazuli "unguent bottle in the form of a wasp" that you were supposed to wear on your shoulder to hold your dress closed. That would be your only ornament. It had ruby eyes and I don't know what-all. We tried to imagine how we could have ever gotten along in Egypt during the thousands of years that insect jewelry was the rage. We imagined ourselves going out and begging the jewelers to make us up a string of pearls or a dinner ring with just one sapphire in the middle and a circle of diamonds around it. We would tell them we'd seen a bug like that in some tall reeds, way down at the source of the Nile, called a "Cartier" bug.

By the time we got up and put our clothes back on, I was all keyed up and happy. I felt I had barely enough time to think about the party and our hairstyles. Of course it would be a great waste, since I'd have to get rid of my marcel before the Chanel show, which was only two days away. Otherwise, it was so dated, they might not let me in. They might think I was an old lady from the Balkans.

"I like to go all in white, don't you?" Jean said. "Though I know it's not quite the thing."

"You should not depend on fashion trickery of that kind, Jean," I said, mimicking the arguments they had used against me when I picked out my white coat. "Elegant people prefer fashion self-knowledge and breeding, always."

Jean was pulling her dress on as I said this, and now she stopped moving and peered out at me from behind the open bodice like a deer in ambush.

Faintly she said, "Is that the kind of thing you say at the store?"

"I was only kidding," I said, taking her hand in mine and feeling terrible. Then I pulled her dress all the way on. She didn't look up at me, but smiled a little and fussed with fastening her belt. "See, it's the way the buyers talk," I said to distract her and myself. "Whenever an important millionaire customer comes in, the buyer comes out, as if by chance, of course, and brags about fashion philosophy. You know, so that they'll buy more."

"Oh, I see," said Jean.

"It's just selling!"

"Does Mr. What's-his-name know? The circus man?"

"Mr. Lazarus?"

"Yes."

"I don't know."

We went to the mirror and looked at our smashed hair.

"We look like two little pinheads," said Jean.

"Let's put towels on our heads," I said. "That way they'll have to fit us in upstairs. They'll *pity* us."

"I've got my Venida Double-Mesh somewhere, but I've only got one," said Jean. "Let's be identical."

We walked out in our towels but with fresh lipstick, so that we felt we made an intriguing spectacle, and on the way I told her about a famous, bossy millionaire woman of Columbus I had seen come into the Paris Salon room at Lazarus's, where the high-priced dresses were sold, and how the buyer had made her buy a bunch of Hattie Carnegie sundresses. She had told the woman about an acquaintance of hers who had bought five or six "to carry her through the season at Juan-les-Pins," and how she would come in straight off the beach, and, adding only a diamond necklace, go straight to an elegant dinner and be the most beautifully dressed woman there. So much more so than the titled Italian woman beside her, who was ever so much richer, but who stupidly believed that heavy brocade was the same thing as distinction! "But I'll bet you anything she never wore those sundresses once."

"Because she was too fat!" said Jean.

"And when she comes back to the Paris Salon, it will be full of brocade dresses."

"What will the buyer do?"

"Stay in her office. No, she won't remember, probably."

We entered the hallway where the shops were, and the Servant of Mankind came up to us with a smile on his face.

"I'd like to show you girls something nice I just received as a gift," he said. He was carrying a white monogrammed scarf. "You see?" he said. "W. N. A. These are my initials. Walter Norbert Adams. But do you know what else they mean? 'Winter North Atlantic.' That's because I'm dangerous!"

"That's awfully smart," said Jean.

Then there was a pause, so I said, "I love a white scarf, summer *or* winter," and was immediately embarrassed.

Though he was distracted by our towels, the doctor went with us to the doorway of the beauty shop. There he left us, after formally saying good-bye by bending over our hands.

The salon was full of customers. It was a pretty room, with lighted pink-glass columns at each corner, and plenty of round mirrors, large enough so that they looked like a row of setting suns. A tall girl with a small face sat at the reception desk near the door, conspicuously idle. She had been watching the doctor take his leave. Before we could say anything, she said, "That one thinks the moon is made of green cheese. And he'll tell you so."

Jean and I agreed.

"But it's not. What have you got under the towels? If you're bald, I can't help you!" Then she smiled good-naturedly.

"Can you fit us in?" asked Jean. "We shampooed it already but we want to get it set."

"If you can wait, I'll do you both," she said, glancing around behind her.

We sat down in some little stuffed chairs covered in pink and green fabric with birds-of-paradise on it, and instantly an angry woman hurried in. She was dressed all in cerise—knitted suit, and high heels as well. She first paused to look us up and down, then wheeled away to the desk. "Simmons College," whispered Jean.

"Just so that you'll know, Miss Slats," she said in an English voice—"Oxford College," whispered Jean—"I have spoken to both the staff officer and the purser about your conduct to me, and, mind you, they are taking up the matter."

Our friend Miss Slats gazed up at her but showed no reaction of any kind. The Englishwoman sighed and went out, not looking at us this time.

"All done up like Astor's racehorse," murmured Miss Slats.

This was a kind of behavior I was used to seeing at Lazarus's, and of course in my view Miss Slats had behaved magnificently.

"Well, she was in this morning," Miss Slats began, her head a little to one side, "and she wanted me to fit her in, and fix her hair like—what's her name . . ."

"Wally Simpson," said Jean.

"That's it," said Miss Slats, pointing at her. "But she didn't like it when I finished. It's a homely style. So she said, 'I'm warning you. You'll get no tip for this hairdo!' It's not as if I didn't know she was what we call a 'piker' by this time. So I just let her complain."

Jean and I took this in.

"But! What she really wanted was a fight. So back she comes with her husband. But he was embarrassed, so they left. *Then* she comes back alone and tells me she will never travel Second Class again, because of the vulgarity of the service. Now, that really raised the old Ned with me. And I had customers waiting. So *I* said, 'I'm sure you'll be better off in Third!' You know," she continued to us, "with the immigrants from Timbuktu."

While we laughed admiringly she said, "Well, I had fun."

Her name wasn't really Miss Slats. It was Roslyn. "Slats" was her nickname, because she could never put on any weight. We had such a delightful afternoon with her. First she refused to give us finger waves, because they were old-fashioned. When we explained about our costumes, it didn't mean anything to her. So we yielded, never even asking what she meant to do instead. Why? It was just an adventure to let a stranger boss us.

While she worked, she talked without stopping. She told us about life on "the Eastern Shore," and about her adventures in her Ford. She had gotten this job through her uncle and was one of only two Americans working on the ship. Before this she had worked in the Catskills, but she liked this better and had saved plenty. But her sister had gone to the bad on

Broadway. She had kicked the gong around. Now she was in a rest home. "What can you do?" she would say bluntly, and Jean or I would say, "Nothing at all," as if we'd faced such problems many times. For my part, I was as ignorant of these things as a person of nineteen can be.

In the end we had side parts and smooth "pageboys" just like every other modish young woman that year. "See, it's better to be glamorous," Roslyn remarked.

Meditatively she brushed out my hair while Jean sat in the next chair, fluffing hers and looking at it from every angle. "You've got a real head of hair there, girl," Roslyn said to me. "Like Dorothy Lamour. You could go like her—in a pinned-up towel. That would be a good costume."

"No," I said.

"Go as Little Egypt, then. I hear she had a thick head of hair, even though that's not what she's famous for!"

"No!" I said, full of dread.

"Maybe your friend Wentworth could get you some pie plates," said Jean. "All you'd need is some pie plates and some string, to look just like Little Egypt."

"For the love of Pete," said Roslyn laughing.

"Why me? Why don't you go as Little Egypt?" I said to Jean. "He's your friend, too."

Jean sighed and stretched and looked up at the ceiling. "Suppose I did, and I put the pie plates on *over* my dress? For a joke on the men, you know."

This struck us funny, and in the end Roslyn had the pie plates sent to my cabin through a fellow she knew in the kitchen. We pounded holes in the edges with a stylus from my sewing kit, and one of Mrs. Trent's tie shoes. It was better than it sounds, because the pie plates were not what we had envisioned, but the small individual size—four in all.

Then we went up to dinner, and I sat alone with those

people I can't remember. I worried a great deal about my own costume and got quite nervous. I was hungry and I ate, but otherwise could barely move. I know I love to go to parties, but apparently I'm not humorous enough to dress up in a costume; at least I never have since. It's too bad—it always disappoints the other people, but I can't help it.

Some time while I was drinking my coffee and staring at the table, Harry appeared and sat down in the chair next to me, where someone had just gotten up. The first thing he did was pretend to be disgusted by the remains on the dessert plate in front of him. He made a big thing of it, but I didn't pay any attention to him.

Then he said, "Where've you been all day?" Then he said, "Where've you been all my life?" and laughed. He leaned on the table and stared into my face.

"I won the pools, you know," he said.

"You did?"

He frowned and sat back, and looked at the dessert plate. "No," he said slowly. "Your friend that fellow Dan did. Say, is it true you're a fashion model?"

"No. Who told you that?"

"I heard it. What *do* you do, then? Everybody's wondering."

"Just because you're wondering doesn't mean everybody's wondering. I work for a department store."

"Oh," he said. "Father own it or something?"

"No."

"Well, how old are you, anyway?"

"Thirty-six."

"Oh, come on," he said, laughing excitedly. "I don't believe that! Ha ha!"

Actually, I was glad Harry had come over and distracted me, but now I stood up.

"What are you going as tonight?"

"I don't know," I said, and I left the dining room.

This time Harry stayed behind, and I went into the library, which was empty. I sat down and wrote a letter to Hattie on the ship's paper. I told her all about the party, trying to explain why I couldn't wear a costume, even though I should, and I knew she would. She would have sewn something from scratch—probably with five or six layers and a complicated flounce, and sewn something for Mrs. Trent as well, and made everybody on the ship happy.

Then I wrote my father and told him about the weather—inventing a story about high winds—and about Dan winning the ship's pool. I told him how I had become friends with the jazz baby, but told him that the jazz baby was actually a married man and not a flirt. I told him I'd had my hair set at a beauty salon and that there was a big ship's party on for that evening.

Five or six people came into the library at that point, making a lot of racket. My back was to the door so I turned around to look.

Ed was leading them, talking loudly, and behind him came the Servant of Mankind, grinning and rubbing his hands. I didn't know any of the others—they were some of the old women that always followed the doctor around.

"Now for the dictionary," said Ed. "Ah, do you have it, *mam'selle?*" he said, coming toward me and speaking in a librarian voice. "Of course not! What would you want with a dictionary? What are you doing?"

"Just writing."

He put one hand on my shoulder and looked down for a moment at my letters. "Well, you can't improve on Fannie Hurst, you know, so don't even try." Then he patted me and went away, saying grandly, "She was like a full moon when she opened her mouth and yawned."

"Here! We found it, Ed!" exclaimed one of the ladies.

I realized that Ed of all people would not expect me to dress up in a costume against my will, and resolved to stay where I was in the hope that the others would leave soon and I could get him to comfort me.

I addressed my two envelopes while Ed won his bet about the word, and soon the group was moving back toward the door, the doctor saying, "I can't get over it, Ed, my boy. But you were right, and by George my word is as good as my bond!"

"We'll see about that," called Ed in a pleasant voice as they all went out the door. He pulled one of the wing chairs up beside me and sat down. "If he's a doctor, I'm a monkey. So don't get sick."

"I won't."

He took out two cigarettes and gave me one, and lit it with a wooden match.

"I'd like to call you Eddie sometimes," I began, since I don't like to talk about my weaknesses and would always rather talk about something else.

"Please call me Eddie. I adore it," he exclaimed. "And I'll call you . . . 'Mary Baker Eddy.' " We laughed a little bit over this, and frankly, I didn't know who Mary Baker Eddy was.

"So!" he then said. "What are you working on tonight? Mystical Essays? Science of Being?" He said this though the sealed-up envelopes were sitting right in front of him, all addressed.

"What did you and Jean do all day anyhow? Your hair looks nice, by the way. Not that it was worth it! You were gone five solid hours. Harry and I got depressed. Harry and I and Cyril, of course, not that we mind about the help. And Jean went off right after dinner to tie her pie pans together so that I can live the rest of my life hiding in the Southern Hemisphere. Who are *you* dressing up as? Use 'Eddie' in your answer."

I took a long time putting my cigarette out, and then I told him I didn't want to dress up at all, in anything.

"Don't then. Who cares?" he said.

"But what about Jean?"

"She won't mind."

"You don't think she'll mind, when she's dressing up in pie plates to look like Little Egypt?" I was so relieved as I said this that I didn't care if he saw I actually had tears in my eyes from nerves. *"I'd mind if it was the other way around!"*

" 'Eddie! I'd mind, Eddie.' "

"I'd mind, Eddie."

"Well, Jean's not like that. Now let me read your letters. I love to know about girls' thoughts."

He picked them up and turned them over. "Ohio! You actually wrote a letter to Ohio?"

"Well, where are you from, then?"

"Ohio!"

I started laughing and Ed said, "Oh, Eddie, you're such a funny fellow. Is this the quaint old gentleman?" he went on, holding up the one addressed to my father.

I said it was, and he took the letter out, unfolded it carefully as if it were a strange artifact, and sank back in his chair to read.

"Thirty-mile-an-hour winds!" he murmured. "Mary Baker Eddy is quite the fabulist!" Then he said with interest, "Who's the jazz baby? Why don't I know him?"

Of course I had forgotten all that part of the letter and didn't know what to say. I just sat there and felt my face heat up. Then he looked at me in disbelief.

"Do you mean to say that I'm the jazz baby?"

"It was just a joke!"

He threw himself back against the cushions, dropping the letter on the carpet, and he laughed for a long time. I laughed, too, though for me it was mixed with embarrassment and sadness for my father's sake.

Soon Ed was sighing and rubbing his forehead. He got out another cigarette and shook his head saying, "You're the mystery girl, all right."

Dolefully I said, "I know I am." Then I said to Ed, "Why don't we go down and see Jean, so I can ask her if she minds?"

"Right," said Ed, lighting up, this time with a swank silver lighter, and we went.

The public areas were empty as we went along. I knew this was the wonderful hush before a party. I prayed I could go and have fun in my regular clothes.

When we got to where the shops were, we went down a hallway at the other end from the one I was familiar with, and this brought us to a lacquered white door, quite different from the door to my cabin.

"Jean! It's Eddie!" called Ed. She laughed from inside— more a scream, really—and I knew she knew I was there as well.

Inside, there were clothes spread out everywhere. It seemed so airy. Their beds were side by side and there seemed to be five or six lamps, all of them on. Jean stepped out of the bathroom, edging around the door gradually like an exotic movie star while Ed and I examined her. She had arranged her pans—there were two on her bosom and two hanging from a long string around her waist—over a floor-length black jersey dress. It didn't look funny at all, it really looked provocative. Ed was chuckling. I took her arm and made her come into the bathroom with me.

"Do you mind if I don't wear a costume?" I whispered, full of dread.

"Oh, I don't care!" she answered, a little bit mystified, I guess. "You could always just be my sister. My good sister. From the convent!"

Ed had followed us. He was kneeling down and fiddling with the pie pan that hung across her bottom.

"Leave it alone, mister," she said, slapping his hand away. Then she turned and said, "But you know, Wentworth is fixing you some pans. I asked him to."

"Oh, I don't know!" I said sadly in a wail.

I went and sat down on the bed, and they followed me back out.

"Just be true to yourself, Mary," Ed said, and he poured us each a little drink from a bottle on the dresser.

"To religion!" said Jean. It was their customary toast.

"To Christian Science," said Ed.

"That's what Ed's mother is," explained Jean. "But she does allow vitamins."

"My Aunt Bessie is one," I said.

"I'll bet she's nice," said Jean, smoothing out her skirt. Ed turned toward Jean. "I was just telling her she reminds me of Mary Baker Eddy," he said, "just before she abandoned the workaday world."

"You know, Ed's mother—"

"Mother Estelle," inserted Ed.

"—Mother Estelle," said Jean, "tried to get *my* mother to take glands for *egg production*, can you imagine? And they've never even met! And *my* mother, who's lived all her life in South Orange, New Jersey, thought Ed's mother thought she was in *farming*, and that kind of thing kills my mother because since they moved to Biarritz she feels so *déclassée*. She would rather live in disgrace among her own kind. But my father wouldn't."

Jean paused and then started again. "I'll tell you *everything*. Her complexion is very wrinkled—more like tissue paper—and it just worries her no end, so when I was showing her picture to Ed's mother (Mother Estelle, who's a Christian Scientist), Ed's mother said that she was 'badly decayed.' And I told her how Mother has to go all over Biarritz—it's the Côte Basque!—in a sunshade with lead particles in it, and how she goes to medicinal spas all over the Alps."

"She was carried to Lourdes in a basket," said Ed.

"But it's right nearby, Ed. Right around the corner," said Jean.

"And that got Mother Estelle's back up," Ed explained.

"Well, let's face it, the whole town is Catholic," said Jean. "So Mother Estelle sat down and wrote my mother in Biarritz about the egg production turning back the clock of time. And my mother didn't know who she was. She's very sensitive and it probably gave her a million wrinkles."

"Well, my Aunt Bessie wears a bellyband, I know," I said.

"Does she?" said Jean. "I just love that name. That would be a dear name, like Bessie Love. Bessie Love Cox."

Ed chuckled. "Why stop there? Why not Bessie 'Loves' Cox?"

I emptied my little glass, for fortitude, and then got up to go. Ed had dozed off, but when Jean went to take his glass he wouldn't let go, so perhaps he was just resting his eyes. Jean came with me, after putting a lipstick in her evening purse, leaving all the lights on, and locking the door to keep the cardsharps out.

She showed no self-consciousness on the long walk to my cabin in her pie pans but told me how at dinner Dan and his wife had come and chatted with them, and Dan's wife had made the steward go get her a Manhattan with a cherry in it! This was disgusting in our view. She also called liquor "alky," which showed us how "Stone Age" she was. She also had licked her finger and *washed her face with it*! But, then, as Jean pointed out, what were any of us but just cats mewing in the kitchen closet? I thought that was very fair of her.

Once in my cabin I took off my white dress and went into the tiny bathroom to bathe and get ready. Jean reclined on my bunk, fussing quietly with her pans and humming. We hadn't been there two minutes, though, when there was a knock on the door and an aged steward appeared with a bouquet of flowers and four pie pans from Staff Captain Wentworth.

Jean took them from him, saying, "Oh, thanks ever so much," while I watched with mixed feelings around the bathroom door. The steward was apologizing for being late.

"You see, miss, Captain Wentworth asked me particularly to have the pans here by seven o'clock, and now it's eight-forty, but they are serving the blancmange, and I had to argue with the cooks, and then the winter garden man is a Tartar. So you see I had my work cut out for me, miss." He put the flowers into a glass. "And yet the man has known me thirty years! So I hope I didn't let the ladies down," he concluded, glancing for one second at me.

"Well, it's just a beautiful surprise," said Jean. "Aren't those gladiators or something?"

"Gladiolus, miss. In the miniature. Straight from Persia. And here, you'll see, the little wristbands," he said, presenting Jean with a little band of satin braid with wire. "You put these on your arms, you see, and there you have corsages, if you so wish, for the party, without troubling the costumes."

"And here's your *gage d'amour* to erase any doubts," cried Jean when the door was closed and she'd flung the pie pans on the bed. "Oh, he's such an Old World man!" Soon I heard her pounding holes in the new pans, "just in case."

I put on my light blue dress, which was similar to Jean's black one, with the difference that hers was made of jersey. Then I went before the mirror, and in a rush of cheery talking she arranged my pans and our corsages.

We stood looking at ourselves. Jean said, "I think I'll just pull this top string a little tighter on you, shall I?—or they might not stay in place."

"They're sliding into my underarms."

"People might think they're dress shields," she murmured. "I doubt if Little Egypt bothered with those. All right. Pull your shoulders back. Don't put your hands behind or they won't see your bouquet. Ha! Good! Now, say 'Mammy.' "

"Mammy."

We patted our hair for another little while and then we went out, Jean slamming the door to give me courage.

When we reached the wide hallway with the shops, we saw a woman coming out of the pharmacy ahead of us. She had scarves knotted in her hair at the hairline, and flowing down behind. She giggled at the sight of us, and we followed her wide behind all the way into the ballroom, to the sound of the orchestra playing "Only Make Believe," which ended the moment we arrived at the double doors.

The room was bright and roaring with voices. The tables were placed all around the edges, and the center was full of dancers. A man in a white apron and a Homburg and dragging a draped tea wagon stopped to offer us "French kisses," and then guffawed.

"I told Dan we'd look for him," said Jean, paying no attention. She started in among the tables and I followed. Most of the noise was coming from the dance floor, the people at the tables having nothing to do but to look us up and down.

I heard a lady say, "Pie plates! Isn't it darling! Look!" and then peals of laughter breaking out around us.

Jean said, "There's Dan's wife. The *charmant oiseau!*" But I looked behind us for some reason, and saw Wentworth out in the hallway, so I left Jean and went back the other way. This time I looked above everybody's heads, and I happened to see the Bolshie leaning on a pillar, under a flaming sconce. She was dressed the same as on other days, but had applied a lot of rouge.

When I reached the doorway, Wentworth was gone, and though I hurried down to the bend in the hall, I didn't have it in me—perhaps on account of my outfit—actually to run up and down calling his name.

Harry, my sentry, was standing there when I got back. He lifted up my hand and had a good look at my corsage.

"Did Eddie give you these, or did the staff chip in? Well, anyway," he continued, "I'm supposed to lead and you follow. Come on to the table," he said, but then didn't move. "You know, I don't care about your secret man friend. What am I to you? Just a poor fool in evening clothes for you to spit on."

"I'm not going to spit on them, you nitwit. Where are you sitting?"

"Over there, with your friends."

Now we looked at each other a moment. Harry's *je ne sais quoi* was set off amazingly by his evening clothes. But added to that was his angry look. I went around him, hoping to locate the table on my own. In the distance I did see Dan taking his seat, mopping his face with a huge handkerchief. I set off, just turning back to get Harry to come. I waved him to follow me, but all he could see was me waving my corsage in his face, so it backfired. But he made his own problems by being spoiled.

He came with me though, because when we got to the

table, a heavy woman I realized must be Dan's wife announced that we were the prettiest couple in the whole room.

"Hooray," said Jean, looking up, then jumping to her feet to show off our costumes side by side. "We are the fascinating Little Egypt! The stripper. You know!" she said, and Dan clapped.

"Imaginative," said Dan's wife in dismay.

"Honey," said Dan to me as we took our seats, "this is Mrs. MacPhinney, or Dora to you."

I said how do you do. Dora told me she had heard all about me, adding, "I've always thought it would be so glamorous to be a fashion model. That's why I love dressing up." She gestured at her bodice and hair, which were covered with dyed feathers.

"Only she's *not* a fashion model," remarked Harry in a cool voice. "She's a salesgirl or something."

"Well, she could be!" said Dan.

"Get her a drink, Harry," said Jean. "The fellow's right behind you."

"I'll have a gin fizz," I said, pulling on the waiter's coat.

"Say, miss," said Jean to me, "you didn't get to see Mrs. Dicky. Black sequins from head to toe. To turban. Queen Victoria, silly!"

"Mrs. Dicky? Dear, is it any relation?" Dora said excitedly to Dan.

"To who?"

"Why, you know. That Harold Dicky that's so near the president!"

"Harold Ickes? Nah," said Dan.

Dora leaned over to me. "Dan's a big shot in Washington. Ask him anything."

"Oh," said Jean. "Is it true that whenever you go to a party in Washington, you have to watch what you say because Mrs.

Roosevelt is either at the table or out in the pantry helping with the dishes?"

Dan threw back his head and said, "Ha ha ha."

"It's incredible to me how any man could go into public life with a name like Ickes," said Harry.

"I like 'Rexford Tugwell,' " I said. "You feel he could do anything."

Harry relaxed in his chair. "Tugwell's a relative of mine."

"That so?" said Dan.

"Yes," said Harry. "Cousin of my father's."

"Well, what do you know."

"Speaking of coincidences," said Dora, "who do you think is on this ship? Why, a girl I went to Normal School with, back in Illinois, and I haven't seen her in twenty years. Rena Howland! I saw her in the salon all dressed to the nines. Had to come down from First Class to get a hair appointment at the last minute. She didn't know me. Why, I'd know her skin drying in a butcher shop!"

"That little woman," said Dan, leaning over and touching my hand, "that little woman there is a saint. She made me what I am today. You'd never think it to look at her, would you?"

"No."

"She's all feminine on the outside, but inside she has the brains of a man. And the steel determination, too."

I was now accustomed to the roaring of the voices and feeling my gin fizz. Dan told a joke I can't remember except for the punch line. It was "Mr. Gimpy, you can mind your own bidnis." It must have been a joke about a shoeshine man.

Then Dora, who was seated next to Jean, turned and started examining her outfit. Soon she was fingering the upper pans, as if she had lost something in there, and the feathers around her head brushed Jean under the chin. We were all watching

in dead silence and fascination. Jean had gone completely
stiff. Then Ed arrived.

"Why, Dora," he began.

"Now see here, Ed," said Dan.

"Ed, you got all dressed up!" said Jean, twisting away from
Dora.

"Oh, that's nothing," said Ed, sitting down between Dan
and me. "So, Dora, what have you been up to?"

With amazing slowness, Dora turned her head but did not
reply. A coldness entered the atmosphere around the table.
It was obvious to all that Dora was completely mad, and that
Dan must lead a life of misery.

Jean turned to Harry, away from Dora, and with bright eyes
asked him for a light from "that lovely Ronson." Of course
Harry's hands were trembling no end.

Dan took Dora off to dance, and Jean said to Ed in a weak
voice, "I'm so glad you suited up. I love to see a man in black
tie."

"Well, then, let me sit there, Harry," said Ed, and soon
Harry was next to me and Ed was laughing and Jean was
exclaiming over the recent drama.

"Care to dance?" said Harry to me.

"I don't want to see Dora."

"That was the most utterly loathsome scene I have ever
witnessed." He was grimacing and practically writhing around
in his chair. "Someone should lock her up."

"Perhaps they didn't really go to dance," I said, wishing to
go dance myself.

"God, no," said Harry. "He's probably tying her up in her
cabin."

The orchestra started up again, and as Jean and Ed were
squeezed up close together, Harry and I went out to dance.
Not only was the floor terribly crowded, but most people had

some kind of thing sticking out—either a broomstick or flapping feathers or a train made out of a tablecloth dragging for yards behind them. Harry held me close and was trembling, and I guess that dance, while we were recovering from Dora, was the peak of my regard and sympathy for him. As the song ended he kissed my neck and my cheek, and then we went back to our table at my insistence. To everyone's surprise, Dan and Dora had also returned in the normal way at the end of the song—Dora's raisin eyes looking out from beneath her royal blue and oxblood feathers. But she was still insane, because when we got back she was slapping at Ed's hand and saying, "Oh, Eddie, don't you high-hat me."

"No, sir, Dora," said Ed. "I'm your man."

Then he turned and asked Harry if he'd gotten anywhere with me.

"Ed!" said Jean, and slapped the back of his head.

"Why is it the women love to slap me?" he said sadly, turning to me. "All except you, Mary."

"Mary!" said Dora, looking around. "I thought her name was Louise. Louise Merrill!"

"Go play the piano, darling," said Jean. "They're waiting for you."

"Right," said Ed, getting to his feet, then bending down to kiss her. "And don't go nutty while I'm gone," he said, embarrassing everyone at the table except Dora, probably.

Somewhere between the table and the stage Ed put on a red plaid winter hat with ear muffs that let down and a strap that buckled under the chin. When he stepped up to the piano, the master of ceremonies was introducing him as "Mr. Ed Cox, the well-known composer of tone poems"—news to me and a complete lie but accepted solemnly by Ed himself. The dancers drifted back to their tables, and we soon had an unobscured view of our hero in his tuxedo and hat, striking a dignified pose with his hands joined before his chest, his face looking pale, and narrow like a dagger.

Some people clapped and laughed, and Ed waved his hand, then said in a loud but melancholy voice, "Act one, Scene one, A Ruined Garden."

He walked round to the bench and seated himself, and began to play beautifully and impressively what was then called "long-hair music," at least that's what I took it to be.

All of us at the table were amazed and impressed, except Jean, of course. The audience was attentive, though there was scattered laughing at his hat. Dan, especially, was overtaken with surprise, and he ran his two hands over and over again through his shiny hair, so that it seemed that if Ed got any better, he would tear it out. Jean smiled at me, and gave a tiny shrug.

He played on grandly for several minutes, no expression on his features and nothing but his hat to remind you that that was Ed up there and not some famous Pole. Once I thought I heard a little melody—I thought it was "I Found a Million-Dollar Baby in a Five and Ten Cent Store"! And then I thought it was "My Blue Heaven." The next thing I knew, Ed was unquestionably playing "It's Just an Old Spanish Custom," still in the same deafening long-hair style. It was an Ethel Merman song. The whole ballroom started roaring and Dora cried, "Don't that beat all!" Dan shouted to Jean that Ed sure was a cutie. I was clapping in time with the rest of the crowd—only Harry was subdued. Even the idle band was beaming at our Ed.

Then there was a long finish, during which Ed brought his face down close to the keyboard and threw it back. The applause was enormous, but Ed barely acknowledged it and then when it died away he began again. This was a little tinkling melody that soon developed into a tremendous boogie-woogie.

A few people started to rise and rush to the dance floor, but then Ed went back again into the little melody, and actually began singing. It was a song he must have written himself, and it ended with

> I want to kiss somebody I like
> So I'll just have to kiss myself.

He stood up and bowed to the applause of all the passengers and orchestra and the discreet smiles of the stewards.

Two bottles of champagne had arrived with the compliments of other tables before Ed even got back to his seat. Dan, though, insisted Ed first drink from his flask of Old Bushmill's, because Dan swore by Old Bushmill's, and then we all had some. We poured it right in on top of whatever was in our glasses already, Dan was so very elated.

Now a big man whose face and hair were moist came up to congratulate Ed and ask him how he got into tone poems. Ed replied suavely that tone poems were just his hobby—always had been.

"And this is your lovely wife, I understand," the man said, looking at Jean. Dora at this point asked him his name—actually, she said, "Who are you?" I think—and the man got down on his haunches and got into a conversation with her. Ed proposed we drink up the first bottle of champagne and then go out and dance. We did, the four of us, with Dan eventually getting up and coming out on the floor to stand partnerless among us. At this point I remembered the lone Bolshie. She was still leaning near the door under the light. I excused myself from Harry and went over to get her, thinking Dan would dance with her if he had no choice. I suppose I must have felt some kind of kinship with the Bolshie and didn't know it.

She deliberately looked away as I approached. "Care to dance with my friend?" I said loudly. She turned her face toward me then, and she looked mad as a hatter. It crossed my mind that this all might not be fair to Dan, what with Dora and everything. She said, "No *thank* you," looking right at me for a weird second, during which I wondered what it was all about. Then of course I turned and went back to Harry.

"I can't see why you bother with a thing like that," said Harry, taking me back into his tight embrace. Dan said, "How 'bout this?" and joined us by putting his arms around my shoulders and dancing with my back. "Say, this isn't bad!" At the end of that song, Dan and I were laughing out of control, and clapping at ourselves. Dan was so good-natured that even Harry wasn't quite himself around him.

The master of ceremonies started yelling out instructions for a novelty dance. By this time listening to anything of the kind was too great an effort for us, and we just stood there panting. When we saw a long line forming around us, we went back to our seats, though Dan looked back longingly once or twice. It was he who spotted Jean and Ed standing face to face out on the floor, with at least two feet between them and terrible expressions on their faces.

I sank down on my chair feeling very shocked. That they should fight suddenly seemed like the ultimate calamity, like the ship sinking. I watched miserably, and saw Jean stamp her foot and rush away, passing our table at some distance. Then she abruptly sat down at a vacant table at the edge of the room. I hurried over there, only to stand with my hands on the back of a chair and watch her cry. Her hands were in her lap and her eyes were fixed on the center of the table, at the harlequin centerpiece with the flowers coming out of its head. I was too stunned in my own mind to think of how to comfort her. Our pie pans and the laughing and the Latin music seemed hellish and insulting with her in front of me like that. That's always the way at parties when something happens.

I wrung my hands, but she just sat on, not sobbing, but motionlessly churning out hundreds and hundreds of tears.

"Do you want a cigarette, Jean?" I whispered.

She nodded. I hurried back to our table and got one from Dan, who looked stricken; I also demanded and got Harry's Ronson, which weighed ten pounds.

Jean was sitting the same way, not looking up, so I put the cigarette right up to her mouth and lit it for her and watched her smoke, praying to God that she might enjoy it and decide to be happy again.

Two gin fizzes arrived without our ordering them. Jean took a deep breath and dried her face with a napkin.

"Trying to be ladylike," she said with a little smile at me. I took one of her hands.

"Oh, your pans!" she said suddenly in almost her normal voice. One of my bosom pans had slid over into the middle. We laughed while I tried to fix it discreetly, but still it was the laughter of condemned martyrs.

Dan appeared and took a seat, bowing first, for some reason.

"Oh, Dan," murmured Jean, shaking her head.

"Aw . . ." he replied in a heartbroken voice.

Jean laid her arm along the table. "Tell my fortune, Dan."

Dan cheered up. "Let's see about that, now," he said, pulling her fingers back to see her palm. "Let's see," he murmured, frowning, "you've got your, you've got your lines . . . let's see . . . ah hah!"

"What is it?"

"First of all, Jeanie, you're going on a trip."

"I am? By sea?"

"Yes, you are."

"Are you absolutely sure?"

"Yes. I can see it right along here."

"But, Dan," I said.

"What, Mary?"

"On her trip—you know—is she going to win the pools?"

"Oh!" said Dan. "Ha ha ha! You two little son-of-a-guns."

"Then what?" said Jean.

"Well," he began again, taking a swallow from my drink, "you're going to reach your destination. No problem."

"Hooray!"

"And, there, you're going to meet a man. A rich man with a great deal of money. But beware!"

"Must be Daddy," said Jean to me.

"And, then, you're going to—let me see—have a little baby!"

Jean and I laughed so loud at this that even in the din twenty or so people turned around to look at us, and then at Dan's soaking shirt and undone red bow tie. To hide, I picked up a menu and started fanning myself. The menu was bound with long colored ribbons and these flew everywhere, just as if I were sending emergency signals when I had hoped to become invisible. Jean and I started screaming all over again.

"I guess you two have perked up," said Dan.

"Dan," I said, "is it going to be a boy or a girl?"

"Well, let me see," he said, going back to his work. "I'm not a specialist, you know. It's just a parlor thing with me I learned back home from my auntie. But let's see here, I don't know. But you're going to have a pretty little friend named Mary . . ."

"For all my days!"

"Yep, for all your days."

"But, Dan, her name isn't really Mary, you know." She

leaned forward and looked where Dan was looking. "Could it be Louise?"

"Her name isn't Mary," said Dan, looking around in surprise. "What is it, then?" he said to Jean.

"It's Louise!"

He looked from her face to mine and then shrugged his shoulders. "I never know when you two are kidding me."

"Quiet, please! No riot, please!" said a voice, and we looked up to see the Servant of Mankind standing there all wrapped up in newspapers.

"I hope I may join you, may I?" he said, taking a seat between Jean and me. "I said to myself, where are the loveliest, most convivial young ladies at this party? I'll find them and sit down at their table."

"I don't guess we've met," said Dan.

"Well, I know who you are," said the Servant, extending his hand. "Walter Adams, Ship's Doctor, M.D."

"MacPhinney," said Dan, shaking hands without the usual heartiness.

"I couldn't help wondering what kind of risqué antics I was missing over here," said the Servant confidentially. "But you all missed great excitement. It was a regular catfight! By the way, how do you like this?" he said indicating his newspaper gown. "One of the ladies had to come to my cabin to pin it on me." He looked down at himself. "It represents the spirit of Gossip."

Dan was getting to his feet. "Don't go, Dan," I said.

"I have to go, honey. See a man about a horse, you know."

"Well, come back afterward," said Jean, "or I might go to pieces again."

"I will, too," I said.

Dan nodded and soon disappeared in the crowd around the door.

"Isn't he just divine?" said Jean, leaning around in front of our companion.

"I know! But just think of . . . Dora!"

"She was *feeling* me! Did you see it?"

"What? What?" said the Servant.

"You're too young," Jean said.

"Well, listen to this, though," he said excitedly. "There is a certain very troubled young woman on this ship with us. . . ."

"The Bolshie," we said in unison.

"Bolshie? I don't know. Really? Well, a young woman, whose father, a well-known big cataract man in Chicago, is sending her to a Viennese clinic. For the insane. She is the most difficult and unpleasant girl alive, and I speak from personal experience, believe me. Now this girl is absolutely forbidden to touch alcohol of any kind, and she is not even allowed to look at it."

"Say!" said Jean.

"That's right, goes completely overboard. Now tonight, what with all the confusion, her attendant lost sight of her. Oh, yes, she has an attendant, all right, but a discreet one, and this mentally ill girl went lurking into the ladies' room, where an elderly woman had left her glass of whiskey by the sink while she went in to—you know. In no time flat this girl sees her chance and drinks it down!"

"Hooray! Howling at the moon!"

"And then this elderly woman, who by the way is the widow of a rich industrialist in Poughkeepsie, New York—she was a Keane—pursued the girl into the hallway—"

"Mrs. Dicky."

"—and confronted her with the empty glass. And this girl called her a quince!"

I burst out laughing.

"What? I didn't hear what she called her!" cried Jean.

"A quince!" said the Servant emphatically. "She said, 'You quince!' But wait! Wait for the best part. Next thing you know they're rolling around on the floor screaming!"

Now he sat back and watched us laughing, with excitement and happiness in his pale eyes.

Jean wiped her eyes and said, " 'Course that happens to us all the time with her. Not that it isn't a good story."

"What? With the insane girl?" he said, amazed.

"No, with Mrs. Dicky," I told him. "She tried to kill Jean one time, you know."

"Did she start it, Louise?" said Jean. "I can't remember."

"Oh, I'm sure she started it," said the Servant gallantly. "But this is amazing! Does anybody know about it?"

"Oh, no," Jean said. "We're used to it, anyway."

"We're professional gunmen," I put in.

The Servant peered at us.

Jean and I were in stitches, but we made no sound. For my benefit Jean put a mean expression on her face, staring at his bent head, and pretended to reach for a gun at her side. At this moment Ed appeared and with one gesture pulled out the vacant chair at Jean's side and sat down and took her hand in both of his.

"Say you love me—lie to me!" he said.

She looked back at him with wide eyes.

"I'm an idiot and should be killed," he continued.

Jean chuckled and gave him her other hand, but shyly. "Don't ever do that again, will you?"

"I won't, I won't. I never will."

"Little lovers' quarrel?" said the Servant, coming alive. "You know, you children have your whole long lives before you."

93

"He's a doctor, see," said Jean, leaning over to me and speaking in a whisper.

They went away to dance, and the Servant—now speaking in a lady-killer voice—proposed we get up and dance, too, to this "bewitching tune." It was a Continental. Much ado about nothing! Soon the Servant and I were standing cheek to cheek, our forward arms extended, waiting for the music to come around. Then we slid out into the crowd, as arrogant as gods. By 1938 everyone knew the Continental; even rural people could do it. But, I will say, the Servant was good at it. He seemed to have taken control of my feet, so that I could just dream. How was it that in profile the Servant looked so forceful—almost like a real man? But, then, why was it that his personality ruined the impression? When it looked out at you, you felt he was practically nonexistent—as if you could steal the shoes right off his feet! "Yes," his eyes seemed to say, "pluck the toupee right off my head and throw it into the sea. Do it right away!"

He dipped me down low and winked as if to say, "I told you I was dangerous," and then, still clasped together, we hurried from end to end of the dance floor. Dad would have had a fit if he saw a "sexless capon" like this winking at me and whirling me around in public. Hattie would say, "Oh, Howard, he's just one of those little wee-wee men."

One of the dancers shouted, "Nuts to you!" and I became aware around then of a certain tension mixed in with the dancing. The master of ceremonies was pointing and cajoling. It was a dance contest and we didn't know it.

"Let's give it our best, shall we?" said the Servant suavely. He kept his eyes on the competition from that moment.

In this contest nobody came around and tapped you when you were out. The master of ceremonies just bellowed out a description of your costume, and when this happened you were supposed to break out into peals of laughter and go sit down. The man who had failed to laugh, and had said "Nuts to you!" had done himself a lot of damage, and now he was standing, abandoned, right at the edge of the floor, and blocking the view of a lot of people at the tables.

Why did they laugh? Just to show that they were uninhibited screwballs, with nothing old-fashioned about them, who'd been disillusioned by the Great War. That was Harry's problem, anyway, or so he told me to my face one time.

"Miss Dance of the Seven Veils . . . and her partner, please!" cried the master of ceremonies. "Yes, who is that? Andy Hardy? Yes, you. Better luck next time. And Statue of Liberty, off *you* go, now!"

"Now how 'bout a hand for our entertaining pianist and his lovely partner in the steel unmentionables, ladies and gentlemen. That's right, thank you very much!" I peeked under our joined arms and saw Ed whirling around a distant part of the floor and clasping Jean tight, neither giving any sign of having heard, though the crowd was giggling in the hopes of a funny remark.

Then the MC went to work on a little package of three couples who were keeping to themselves to one side. One by one he picked them off. "Now Mr. Whatdoyoucallit, if you and your lovely milkmaid will take your bows with our thanks! And will all ice cream vendors and gypsies clear out, too, and we'll bring this happy party to a close." These six all burst out in merry laughter and went away, leaving only the Servant of Mankind and me, and Ed and Jean. The Servant's grip tightened as the song wound up and finished. The MC ran to the piano and with one finger played "The Star-Spangled Banner." There was a burst of laughter and applause, and the Servant stepped back, holding my hand high between us, and then bowed.

95

"How can you win, since you work on the ship?" I said, bending over and speaking into his ear.

"Please! Please!" he whispered, quickly straightening up.

I was given a little tin plate with the date engraved on it, and the words "The *Berengaria* Costume Ball." Soon my partner was borne away from me by some of the ladies who always hung around him, and Ed and Jean came and rescued me. We had a hurried last drink bunched up together at the old table, though Dan and his wife were gone and Harry had vanished a long time before.

"Just think, this time tomorrow," I said.

The bar was closed, so Ed poured out the red wine someone had been drinking before the champagne arrived.

"Drink this," he said. "It's the imprisoned laughter of the peasant girls of France. Now, Louise, a toast," he went on. "Louise! You're a good kid and I'm all for ya!"

We held our glasses up high for a moment, and then we drank. Waiters were working on the tables at the edges of the room. The band was standing up and there was only one other party still seated, and they were singing something.

"Louise," said Jean. "You look like the last grave! The one over by the willow!"

"Well, don't you know why I look that way?"

She looked surprised for a second, then got her hankie out of her purse, and eyeing me, held it halfway up to her face.

"You know," Ed began, "this world would be a better place for children if people didn't drink, but just smoked reefers."

"Ed," said Jean, "are you sure you don't want to go back to Boni and Liveright's?"

"I'll say," he replied. Though still himself in other ways, Ed was no longer conversing normally.

"Well, I hope not," said Jean. "Louise, why don't you sleep in our cabin tonight, and that way we can keep our dreams alive and put off the morrow. To the bitter end. Because you're the first sister I've ever had; though I *do* have a brother."

"I'm an only child," I told her, and then watched her tired-looking eyes fill up with tears. Then, collecting myself, I said, "If I don't want to sleep in your cabin, will you walk me to my cabin?"

"No," said Jean solemnly.

"Well, then, I will."

"Hooray!" And now, beaming and rubbing his hands together, Ed exclaimed, "We can have an orgy! A real holocaust!"

Ed stood up, then the two of us stood up, and we made our way around the table, only pausing to wave at the stewards, specks in the sea of litter. Probably they were sick to death of us.

Once inside their cabin, Jean and I each took a bed. Ed slept between us on the floor in a pile of bedspreads, after shaking hands with me. When we turned off the lights, he began to sing songs like "I Ain't Got Nobody," and bits from his concert, and he called for one of those luggage stickers that say "Not Wanted in Stateroom." He wanted to put it on his forehead.

I WAS THE first one to wake up that morning. Since I was still wearing my dress, I only had to pick up my purse and leave. Probably I looked gruesome and strange. I might have been still drunk, too. As I went along to my cabin, hearing the steam whistle and seeing the bustling people, I felt I had set my foot at the top of a slide, and I was going to regret it. I'd get going fast and soon I'd be in Europe—a Lazarus employee, among strange foreigners and smart alecks.

My dim, tiny cabin looked sweet to me again, just the way it had looked when it was all mine, at the beginning. Mrs. Trent wasn't there—she was probably at luncheon—but all her belongings were neatly packed and ready for the steward. One of these was a carpetbag made of flesh-colored fabric, which leaned against her pillow just like a bosom without a head and kept me company.

During my shower I tried to remember all the things I had to do that day, but only scared myself. I got out and dried myself for the last time with the SS *Berengaria* towel, then spent a churning moment before the open wardrobe. What would Mrs. Eve Harriman wear? How did she pick her clothes so that they said to the world, "I'm an American, in the best sense of the word"?—in this way making everyone at *Vogue* magazine proud?

In the end I wore my dark blue dress and blue pumps, and carried my peek-a-boo hat. I hoped to be ready for the chic Frenchwoman, who had style as a birthright. I also had a daring lipstick, which I used for the first time that morning. It came in a padded silk box with a pattern of Chinese dolls on it. Lazarus's ordered these from Hungary. Mine was called Pigeon's Blood. I wanted it to make me look like Hedy.

I left four dollars for the steward, and tied the little tickets to my luggage. Then, taking my purse and my white coat, I went up to the dining room.

Only four or five tables were occupied, and those by people in their traveling clothes. I ordered waffles from the one steward, but then I could only eat a few bites. The ship was my home, especially this dining room with its staid paneling and the lampshades that seemed so vulnerable to sea disasters. All I could do was look around and wonder what I was coming to. The steward came along and looked over my plate—then, without a word, he just poured my coffee and went away again, proving to me that the voyage was over.

After the still dining room, the atmosphere on deck seemed frenzied with the wind and sunlight. I did not look over the side, but went straight to my chair, which was folded up tight. Charles came around the corner.

"Good morning, miss. So this is it."

"Yes, hi," I said confusedly. I was putting his tip in the ticket slot at the top of the chairback. "This is for you, if I ever get it in here."

"Thank you," said Charles.

"Did Mrs. Dicky ever tip you?" I said, straightening up and facing him, only to have my hair blow straight across my face.

Charles smiled sweetly. "I think she changed her mind about me."

"After you told her you'd kill for half a quid, whatever a quid is. Maybe that did it."

"Oh, I don't think so," he said modestly.

"Well . . . I guess I've got to go now."

"I wish you a successful trip. Will you be coming back with us by any chance?"

"What? On this ship? I don't know." I walked away quickly. In one week I could be right back here on this deck, waiting for my bouillon to arrive!

I rushed back down to the lounge. There I saw all of Second Class—drooping and lounging on the tufted chairs. A couple of people were crying. I saw Mrs. Dicky standing like a soldier by her bags, and she had a loathsome fur hat on her head, shaped just like the cap on an acorn.

The purser stood behind a grillwork window and called out names in a languid voice, while his helpers hurried among the passengers. Once, to my surprise, Wentworth's face appeared at the window, too. He soon left by a side door and was drifting toward the shops, but then must have seen me, because he changed course and came over.

"And so, miss?" he said, reaching out for my hand. "Have you had a satisfactory voyage?" He tilted his head. "Or was it rather dreary?"

"Oh, it was on the dreary side. For someone like me."

Wentworth nodded. I was thinking how debonair he was.

"For someone who's used to what I'm used to . . . it wasn't exactly exciting," I said cleverly. "You don't catch me crying."

"Why should you cry? It's half the stewards who are wetting their pillows this minute. I'll have to go down to the engine

100

rooms, just to muffle my sobs. Have to keep up the side—for the sake of the men, you know. Now, listen," he said, reaching into his lapel pocket, "this here—don't the Americans say that?—this here is the card of a friend of mine in Paris—he's on the spot, which means a great deal, you know—and he'll help you if you should need anything. He's just a businessman, but he speaks the lingo. All right?"

"Thank you."

"Is it a deal?" he went on in a gangster voice.

"Yes, thanks."

"Well, now, good-bye." He took my hand again and put both of his around it. After doing something between a smile and a laugh, he walked away.

"I'm coming back on this ship, anyway," I called out, and at that he turned halfway and waved.

It seemed that all of the passengers had decided they didn't like traveling by sea after all, and that the purser was stealing their money. This made a constant complaining and hubbub. Meanwhile I was thinking that if Jean and Ed didn't come soon, I might never see them again, as I was going on the train and they were being met. I reached into my purse for a little French phrase book Hattie had given me. It was called *Toi et moi.* I had never opened it, and now I would pay! It would be just as she predicted: I'd be wandering around saying, *"Où est moi?"* and the French would find it very *piquante.* I put the book back.

A man sitting in the chair next to where I was standing patted my arm. "Here, sit down," he said in an English voice. I did sit, but facing the other direction. But he was puffing away on a cigarette and I wanted one.

"I wonder if you'd give me a cigarette."

The man wrenched around in his chair to get at his pocket. He was nice and I was so rude! I felt like grabbing his hands and saying, *"Où est moi?"* Our eyes met above the flame and both of us chuckled.

"Good old tobacco!" he said, resettling himself. He was happy and ruddy, like the soldier in *Dawn Patrol*, where he whistles for his imaginary dog.

I felt a tap on my shoulder, and now I turned around to the sight of Jean, glamorous in a pale blue suit that was strangely set off by dangling Bohemian earrings that didn't suit her.

"Aren't these just . . ." she began, moving her head back and forth. "And guess who gave them to me! The battle-ax!"

She grabbed my shoulders and whispered into my ear. "These are Indian earrings, and they have little Nazi signs—it's just a coincidence. She admitted that was why she gave them to me—afraid to carry them into France! She's a go-by-ground, don't you think?"

"I do, I do," I said, laughing.

"So now I just want my father to see them for a second."

"Did you tip everybody?"

"Oh, I've been all over the ship, and then when I find them I never know how much!" She paused and pushed my hair back off my face. "You look different, you know, but I can't tell . . ."

I held up my cigarette. "Also, I'm wearing my Hungarian lipstick. Like—"

"Like what? Like blood?"

"Like Hedy Lamarr," I said, looking at the floor.

"Well, you *do*, Louise, you really do. Oh, have you seen Wentworth? I haven't."

"He gave me his friend's business card in Paris."

"Oh, I'm going to miss you like, like gangbusters—especially when I'm getting fatter and fatter and sitting around Biarritz with the Progress Club. I'll just think of you having dinner

at the Ritz in your pinwheel hat. Oh, I'm so nervous. I wish
we were going on the train, especially when I think of my
parents. Where is Ed?"

"He the red-haired chap?" asked the man in the chair. "I
just waved him over."

"Oh, thanks," Jean said absentmindedly. She sat next to
me and looked me over. "You look awfully good. That's a
smashing coat. *Très elegante.*"

I thanked her.

"But I don't envy you those dry cleaner's bills, Mary," she
said in an old lady's voice.

"I guess I'll regret it one of these days, and I'll remember
what you said." We laughed at ourselves, but then the people
began to move. "What time is it, *monsieur?*" she inquired of
the man in the chair.

"Just a quarter past three," he replied. "Time to get into
line and get it over with."

The crowd was very dense around the door, and fresh air
was blowing into the lounge. We spotted Dan at the other
end, and when he saw us he clenched his fists and waved
them together above his head. Then he waggled his index
finger at us, and blew us each a kiss.

I cried " 'Bye, Dan!" and he answered " 'Bye, honey! See
you in Paree!"

We turned back to get into line. I was trying to shield my
hat when I was pushed from behind.

"It's Ed," Jean murmured.

He gave me another shove. Now the line was moving fast
and there were stewards all along it, politely asking to be let
in or let through. Jean and I were quiet, but most people were
talking and using their loudest voices—mostly to say "I hope
this" or "I hope that."

At the top of the gangplank, the line stopped moving. Ed put his arm around both of us and we just stood there blinking—too blinded to see anything of the land.

Jean twisted around to look into the water below us. "Oh, I . . ." she began.

Neither Ed nor I could see what she was staring at. I shook her arm, but she didn't straighten up. Something in the water had her perplexed.

"Say what it is," said Ed, and she let herself be pulled back from the rail. We stared at her, and so did the people behind us, as she pushed the hair back off her face and blinked.

"It's a box floating down there, that's all, but I didn't want to look in it so I came back up." Then she paused, and said, "Because it might have kittens in it."

Ed and I started laughing, and after a moment she started laughing, too. The line was moving—it was steep, but you had to go on—and soon we were hugging and kissing on the land. Ed whispered, "I gave Harry the name of your hotel, so be prepared. I had to, he offered me money! You know where we are if you get lonely, Mary!" he shouted at the end, and Jean blew me several kisses, while a uniformed man led me to a tall archway that said "Paris." I shook him off and turned to see my friends just vanishing.

I saw sheds and smoke and yelling porters—all completely unreal, and the ground heaved me up and down. A line of passengers was coming my way and I had to move. It's just as well, or I would have kept on trying for one more glimpse of them, even if it was just the back of Ed's head, and if I had ever stopped moving during those first minutes on shore, it's probable I might have started thinking things over, and then who knows? All night on the pier on my suitcase, just staring over this way. Crying *Où est moi?* to the gulls. Then, as Hattie would

104

say, a short walk east till my hat floated, or in this case west.

When I picked my suitcase up, a smiling porter was there and he was reaching for it, too. He was the first real native I had ever gazed at. Probably he spoke no English and had never even heard of the United States. Both of us straightened up empty-handed, and I shook my head and waved my hand at him. Then I added, "G'wan!"

I passed through an archway into the building where Customs was. The whole thing was covered with cinders and had never been cleaned. I didn't have to wait two minutes. A man standing idle behind a counter nodded at me, then looked away as if it was none of his business whether I walked to him or flew over. When I arrived, he said, *"Mademoiselle."* Another man lifted my case onto the counter, which was like a long varnished desk from elementary school—it reminded me of getting grabbed and spanked. The first one stood back so I could unlatch it, and then he lifted the lid and looked over the surface of my salmon-colored robe, ignoring the cosmetics that were stuck in around the sides.

"Bon!" he said severely, and nodded, too, as if to say that no inspector could do more, however many illegal items might get through. The assistant fastened the catch and I walked away toward the dark end of the building, toward a lot of French yelling and hissing of trains.

I went self-consciously, too, feeling that unpleasant thing about France. They size you up all the time, and that's the women as well as the men. You may think you're walking to your train or down the street to buy a paper. But they think you're on the prowl for Frenchmen—and that includes old crippled ones, wounded in the war by the Hun—and that you'll even try to tempt those impoverished ones in the knitted caps, whose families are at home just waiting for some food.

If you say you didn't see them, they'll just say, "For shame!" All this I began to perceive during my short visit to Customs that day. I was very conscious of my shoes!

I was helped into the handsome train. It looked like a row of lacquer boxes—not a bit like the Penn Central—and found my way to a compartment, after assuring myself there was no such thing as a normal car in the whole train. It was packed— they were all packed—and just like a horrible small living room. An Englishman was talking, so we all stared at him. He handed around pictures of his little racing dogs.

"This one here's Dainty Man," he said tenderly. I dozed and thought of my ship friends, my face turned to the wall. How inferior this bunch was!

It was pitch-dark and humid in Paris. I walked out of the station, feeling like I was a ghost. I did notice that the people were still speaking French, much the same as at Cherbourg, and that was all I noticed.

I went in a cab to my hotel, the Élysée Palace, rue de Marignan. It was Mr. Lazarus's own favorite. In my room, practically asleep, I dressed for bed and ate a sandwich sent up by the deskman.

I remember these things, but I don't remember my reactions to them. M. Danon, who was the manager, used to love to tell me in later years how I acted that night.

"But sullen and unpleasant, *mademoiselle*! 'Poor Mr. Lazarus,' I said to my wife."

A letter had come for me from Hattie, and someone had playfully left it on my pillow.

Honey,
    I am writing you now so you'll have something to meet you when you get to the hotel. I hope they'll put this right on your pillow.

I don't want you to feel strange over there just because you're in a new place. I know it's awfully hard on a person to go on a long trip like you have, and then land all alone in a big city—sort of that *"Où est moi?"* feeling, isn't it? But it's just because you're tired. You know I never got over that way you feel the first day or so. And then it's normal to get a case of the jitters the first morning. I always did. I would just lie there in my strange hotel bed perspiring, and I'd make vows to be good if the Lord would take me out of it and take me home. Or I'd vow to become a Roman Catholic. But by dinner I'd be myself, and calling to the people at the other tables, and so will you.

Red is here by my chair running in his sleep. He's awful nutty. He misses you already, almost as much as I do. He pulled the sheets off Mrs. Wilmot's line while I was at work today, and then ran around barking with them on his head. I guess he wanted to make sure the neighbors knew he was the one that did it, so they could inform Mrs. Wilmot. So I spent the evening washing them with a cake of naphtha soap. That soap took me right back through the years to 81st Street when your father and I used to try to carve it into animals for our Noah's Ark. I couldn't tell Mrs. Wilmot I don't generally do my own wash. My, I never saw such sheets. They were just like canvas. Now they're hanging on the curtain rods to dry. Red's been staring at them.

Mrs. Wilmot met me in front of the house, and when I got out of the car—I was working late and I hitched a ride with Mr. L.—she couldn't help saying, "My, but that's a doozie of a car!," mad as she was.

Did you hear about your father's cousin Phillip? He crashed a plane and broke some ribs. He says it wasn't a crash, but a "Chinese three-point landing." And the same day it happened, his brother's name was in the newspaper! It said, "What

New York boy is that way about film starlet Ella Something?"
Your mother says your father was embarrassed all day. But I
don't know why since he claims he hasn't seen them since
1927.

I suppose you'll hear all about it before you go.

You made a wonderful impression at your farewell party. Mr.
Lazarus laughed till he cried when you and your pal wrapped
up all the hors d'oeuvres like two little girls at a picnic. I've
written your mama all about it. She's so proud of you, even
though she fusses at you. It's just some people's nature to worry,
dear.

Well, I better wind this one up. Don't you worry about the
business side. It's going to be as easy as pie, and whatever you
decide to bring back, it won't be wasted. I've had several ladies
hinting to me about the Paris gowns you're going to bring back
with you, and Mrs. Vincent Jones is all ready to go on a diet!

Have as much fun as you can and if you need anything, the
man in the hotel will help you. I can't remember his name but
I understand he'd walk on tacks for any friend of Mr. Lazarus,
just like all of us.

I've sure enjoyed writing this, almost as if we'd had a nice
little visit and you were still right around the corner. I'll write
again tomorrow. "Course I ain't no *Guy de Mopassong!*"

> Hugs and kisses
> Hattie

I didn't wake up until noon, when a maid entered the room.
She came right in, carrying a tray, and looking around her
with eyes like pinheads. She looked into my suitcase as she
walked by it, and at the label in my coat, which was thrown
over a chair, not even checking first to see if I was looking.
She set the tray down on the bedside table—still as if I weren't
there—and screamed, *"Le café, la brioche, le newspapaire!"* She

then made the coffee from scratch, or so it seemed to me, out of several steaming pitchers. It didn't give me that party feeling, though.

Her lips were gathered into a tight little knot and held that way, so I bunched mine up, too, and stared at her that way from my pillow. For Jean's benefit, I guess.

Still without looking my way, she picked up the phone receiver, handed it to me and walked out. I lay there, and soon raspy sounds came in. M. Danon was on the other end, sending me good wishes.

"*Une belle invitation* for this evening, *mademoiselle*." Gradually I made out that some couturiere was asking me to dinner. He said that I needn't even call her back if it was after all possible for me to go. In that case I should just "go and be happy!" I thanked him and hung up the phone, which was shaped just like a wrench.

So the designers were trying to get around me—to wine and dine me, to get in with Mr. Lazarus and Federated Department Stores, all of which were chic, and profitable. So now it would be carriage rides through the Bois, and blandishments. Every night *chez* Maxim's. What would I do if they offered me cut rates, lower than the worst ready-mades, expecting me to buy in the thousands, when really I had a budget for one model from each? I would refuse, of course, and then the *tout Paris* would laugh at me, and read about it in the paper. The baby on the man's errand. Hattie would lose her job. I would slink around Cherbourg, never taking a bath, until I died and they sent me home horizontal—in a simple pine box.

Stomping around the bed I remembered asking Hattie if this might happen and she'd said it couldn't. Born yesterday Hattie! Just flew in from Philadelphia. As if Patou and Chanel wouldn't know about Lazarus's and the great man who ran it. Hadn't he called FDR on the phone one day, and settled it that Thanksgiving would fall on the third Thursday of every November? Wasn't he the father of revolving credit, and wasn't I his deputy and perhaps in some way a representative of the President, too?

The possibility made choosing my outfit harder. And I had other things on my mind, such as what about taxis and how do you flag them down in this city?

I had one hour and fifteen minutes to get to the Chanel rooms on the rue Cambon. I jumped into the bath (there was a real bathroom and I thought nothing of it, being ignorant), then jumped out and powdered myself until you couldn't see in there. Bypassing everyday lipsticks, I reached for the box from Hungary. With my hand shaking, I put it on my mouth and some on my cheeks—Mrs. Roosevelt's reservations notwithstanding.

I got into my navy blue dress after all. It was the only thing I had that wasn't rolled up, and as I dashed around the room carrying my hairbrush and my shoes with me, I harassed myself about the couturiere and who she might be. Would it be Schiaparelli, and would she make me look at her shrunken-head collection, and her famous monkey hats? Well, I'd pay no attention. I wouldn't wear stockings. And I wouldn't yield about my dresses either, however she might scorn me, or insult me to my face in French, when I just thought she was being nice. If it got too bad, I concluded, I would go to the Bonwit Teller office and hide out as Hattie had done on her trips over here. My mother had a pack of letters from her on Bonwit's stationery—long stories about visits to the Ritz bar with different Americans named Bill.

I hadn't even looked out the window yet—fear of seeing something that might intimidate me—but now I couldn't help noticing the air outside was bright and hot. I'd have to leave my coat behind, but I'd make up for it with my red high heels. Hattie didn't like them. They let strangers see my instep. But they might impress "Schiap."

I had thirty minutes to get to Chanel. I ran to the birdcage elevator and it slowly wobbled down. I had no recollection of the lobby when I saw it, nor of M. Danon, who called to me from behind the desk.

"*Veuillez attendre, mademoiselle.*"

Why did I ignore him and hurry on toward the street door, clutching my purse and staring at the faded carpeting? "You were just like a soldier!" he said later, shaking his head.

It was bright and dusty in the street, with roaring cars and men yelling all around. M. Danon came through the doors, and while I stared, he caught at the card in my hand that was my invitation. He ordered a man to get a cab, then handed the card back to me with an envelope. A cab pulled up and he half-crawled into it. When he backed out he winked at me and said, "Please get in! He will take you to the rue Cambon." Why had he winked?

But as we jerked away from the curb, I started to get a little bit of that party feeling. An old man rode beside us on a bicycle, with breads sticking out of his knapsack at all angles. He was traveling twice as fast as the cab, and yet he looked too skinny to live. And I saw "Tonique" signs on all the buildings, and clouds of dust.

Soon another cyclist was alongside us—a younger man who peered in at me. When the cab stopped at a crossing and he stopped, too, I slid down in my seat and closed my eyes to slits. What if he was pressing his face against the window? I covered my face with my two hands. When we started to move, I looked around. He was far away—way up ahead and pedaling. Just as if I didn't exist!

I suddenly felt so exhilarated I had to get out my invitation and stare at it. Hattie had gotten it somehow. Hattie didn't even care for Chanel.

I remember once telling Hattie the reasons why I liked Chanel and she said those were all the reasons why she *didn't* like Chanel. She actually preferred the House of Edie Purvis, known to all as a third-rate manufacturer who managed to get high prices by making clothes fussy. They had pansy appliqués, loops on the sleeve to hold your hankies, and things like scalloped hems with scalloped petticoats attached. But scalloped with a different-color thread! Hattie thought they were awfully pretty, and also they represented steady salaries for poor immigrant women. Women from places we couldn't even pronounce, but who spoke to us in the international language of sewing! That was Hattie. She didn't care about a fireball genius. Nor did she care for the works of Mme Vionnet, the celebrated architect of fashion and queen of the bias cut. She laughed at all the supposed sacredness of France. And, needless to say, quite a large group of well-to-do Columbus women agreed with her. They could be seen glancing haughtily into the Salon Room on their way to Better Dresses to buy. An article once actually appeared in the *Columbus Dispatch* about the delusions of Paris. It explained the fineness of the new machine embroidery, whereas in old-fashioned Paris they still did it by hand.

Whenever a shipment of her favorites came in, Hattie loved to take me into the storerooms and make me look—through her glasses—at the invisible seams or the edging on a ruffle. She would explain how it was done by hand, and then how the machines did it. She knew the exact number of bobbins and she knew who made the machines, and the machines were always made in Rhode Island, it seems to me now. Hattie felt that machines produced more justice for the working women, by giving them mobility. And she felt that fifty seamstresses were more easily jammed into an unsanitary attic than fifty machines and their operators.

These conversations filled me with tension, I was so afraid that thinking about working women would remind Hattie of her lifelong obsession, the Triangle Shirtwaist fire of 1911, which had happened when she was twenty years old. She was still living with her parents, while she worked for B. Altman. She wasn't at the fire. Her only connection with it was that she read about it in the paper, and that the victims sewed and she was in retailing. But it hit her very hard. My father said that from then on she used to read everything she could find about catastrophes and working conditions, and she used to send boxes of B. Altman clothes all around the city.

She introduced me to the story when I was about eight years old and it agonized me for several years. Hattie was cheerful, unlike my mother and father, and the sight of her face streaming with tears, along with her explanation of the *inevitability* of each girl's fate when it came has marked me for life, as well.

I spent my next few childhood visits wondering when this side of Hattie would come pouring out of her again. Once while I was working with her in Columbus, there was a terrible fire in a Woolworth's not far from the store. I so dreaded her finding out about it, but I had to be the one to tell her in case she went to pieces at the news. I wasn't going to let someone else see her and fire her for insanity. When I reached her office, she was standing stiffly at the window, and I could hear what sounded like twenty sirens down in the street.

"Hattie," I said.

"Where's the fire, dear?" she said. When I told her she

went back to her desk and closed her eyes, only remarking that at least nowadays there was such a thing as a fire code to protect people.

It was her preoccupation with the fire that led her parents to arrange her vacation (not expecting her to go all the way to Santa Fe, New Mexico, and become a squaw, of course).

When her things came to me after her death, I expected to find a great deal about it and its aftermath, but there wasn't anything like that. It was almost all clippings of ancient fashion news pasted into books, including a whole portfolio on Worth. The clippings petered out after 1920 or so. By that time Hattie was thirty years old and too busy in Columbus to care what somebody else might think about clothes.

But regarding the fire, she had something memorized from the newspapers. She told it to my father once in a low moment and, according to my mother, he thought about it, too, in the middle of the night. But she wouldn't lower herself to ask him what it was. I know she would have rather he was haunted by something of *hers*.

There was a crowd in the side street we entered. The driver said something to me that sounded like "Boom, boom, boom." Then I saw the name "Chanel" on a metal plate by the door. So, these were the mobs I'd heard about who live for fashion but have no job. The ones who'd commit murders for the sake of fashion; to get the world to give up peplums or tiered skirts. I'd heard about it from Ellen Schutz, the buyer. She disapproved, but she was kind of the same herself, to the point of sneering, if not murder.

The driver nosed us in as far as he could, then said, *"Eh voilà, mademoiselle."* I gave him some money on the willy-nilly system—that's the name Jean gave it. "Just give them something and see what happens." Actually, he gave me some back.

Though the crowd was all around the car, they were looking not at us but toward the small door. There were random thuds on the roof and hood. I climbed out and stood, my arms folded around my purse. No one tried to get it from me.

It was now twenty minutes after two. The doors would probably open late, on account of Mlle Chanel's waywardness. But what did she do? Opened the doors suddenly before our eyes—someone did, anyway, and spoke in a voice that there was not a chance of hearing in the yelling of the crowd.

This woman, who was tall and correct but sort of dry-looking, nodded to me and some others. It felt like a dream. We were allowed to move forward. I pushed along to the steps and into the crowded vestibule. The howls rose in volume as the door shut.

My invitation was still in my purse. No one had even looked at it. I suppose whoever wasn't screaming was invited in.

Everywhere I saw drooping hats with veils, lots of diamonds, purple gloves, appalling dressy suits, and plenty of Pan-Cake—all this in early September.

We were ushered into the soft beige salon, to the groups of little hard chairs that were arranged on three sides of the platform at the bottom of the stairs.

"Just my luck," said a woman beside me. She was shoving me toward the wall as we walked.

"What next?" she added.

I walked faster, straight to an inferior seat at the back. I thought I was dumping her, but she came after me and sat down. She sighed as if in despair. I stared straight ahead, while she looked me over. I didn't see why I couldn't be left alone like other people, or even have fun once in a while.

The woman grunted and moved her legs around, but they were fat and didn't bend. She looked like Mabel Normand. In fact, she looked like Fatty Arbuckle!

"Take that hat off before it annoys people." She was nodding. "That's a rule I make."

I looked past her, as if I was expecting a friend.

"At least you're American," she went on more lightly. She bent down and looked at my shoes. "Or since when do they sell those anywhere in Europe? Claire McCardell! Expensive! Who do you work for?"

I jumped up in desperation, but I couldn't see any other seats now, even back where we were. The seat to my left was empty, but I knew there was nothing to keep her from moving over one either. Even if I put my purse there, she would just sit on it.

"Who sent you here to see the modes?" she demanded.

"Lazarus's."

"Oh, the Federated!" she cried. "Federated Department Stores. And Lazarus, of course. Very strong in housewares and all that kind of thing. Not exactly a byword in fashion. Of course, Lazarus himself is a top business leader."

She didn't seem to want a reply and I didn't give her one.

A woman in a wide-shouldered suit—Schiaparelli, I sensed—was standing right in front of me, looking all around before sitting. When she sat, she got out her Dorine pressed powder and went to work on her face. I leaned forward and I saw myself in the mirror. I could do this because I am tall. I saw the face of Mabel Normand flash by, too.

She put her cheek against mine. "You don't mean to tell me," she whispered, "that he's buying direct from Paris in 1938! Why, he practically owns five or six manufacturers I could name, and Weinburg is one of them!"

I covered the right side of my face with my hand and looked

toward the wide staircase, which was lined with long panels of mirror. I felt her mystification growing and soon expected that terrible question: "Say, who are you, anyway?"

She squinted on and on at me awhile, then seemed to forget all about it. I began to feel real happiness. This was Chanel. Chanel always had my devotion—over all of them. I thought I was a *garçonne* type, for one thing, and for another I believed that only Chanel had "real design integrity." In fact, it was the fashion to think so.

There was no talking, and young women in gray moved around mysteriously. What were they doing? They were more like Pinkertons! First we were handed little slips of paper for marking down the numbers of the dresses we liked, and then a tired-looking woman said a few words from behind us— neither loudly nor softly—and what those words were I don't know. Mabel Normand folded her legs and kicked me with her heel. Perhaps she was in pain, because she was rubbing her big, wide ankles. Now *I* recognized *her* shoes. It was a day Betty Wheeler had shown me all the worst shoes in her department, and they were all the biggest sellers, too. We would creep around a certain shelf, Betty in the lead, and she'd point at the particular shoe, her hand flashing in and out like lightning. And after I had looked for a second or two, we'd clutch hands and our eyes would pop. Then we'd turn and look at them again, and they would be all mottled, and with false buttons hiding elastic panels. They were those supposedly flirtatious "pumps" with two-inch-wide straps that would never wear out in generations of wear. Or else they were called "dancing shoes," which meant Cuban heels. Farm women would buy them, and would still be wearing them when they were old, but over thick socks.

I wished so hard that Betty could see a little film of me there at Chanel in Paris, the fountainhead of *haute couture*, seated next to a big pair of Stetson Tailorites, the ones with the big brass eyelets and the cunning open toe! And, moreover, her toe was sticking way out.

Then a woman came quietly down the stairs in a pure white wool shantung dress with a navy flannel jacket over her arm. The waist was the kind of waist no imitator could achieve, and if you wore a corset, you would look like a tree trunk. So you just couldn't be fat, regardless of what Mlle Chanel might say about freedom and comfort and individualness. Oh, my, Chanel's clothes made you want to slouch and cuss, and act like the girls in Chicago, as we New Yorkers pictured them. That is, we thought they left the orphan asylum merely to become the kept women of bootleggers, and to spend their allowances at Chanel. That was the last word among mistresses—looking boyish. That's what they did with their boyfriends' moola, and that's certainly what I'd have done, if I'd had any. Her clothes were my ideal. Hers were the only ones that could take you through every moment of your life. You don't want to visit wounded soldiers' bedsides with your head in a turban, or with your head rising up out of a bunch of stiff ruffles. You want to look like you could help him turn over in his bed. You don't want to look like a snake charmer one minute and Helen Wills the next!

It's still the same look at Chanel—some years better than others, but generally when number one comes down the stairs, all us old buyers still get that happy mood and find ourselves later on having to justify all those orders.

The next two dresses were cotton jersey with V necks, and I marked them down with difficulty, as the woman beside me tugged away at my arm. A man had taken the seat on the other side of me. I looked to see one of the Pinkertons standing over him. I saw her snatch his little paper away and then march off.

"What's he doing?" said Mabel Normand, practically yelling. I swatted at her and she sat back, so I turned to look at the man. He happened to be glancing at me. The whole room was looking, but he wasn't shy. He stared right back at me. I had to blush.

"What'd he do?" shrieked the woman.

He smiled at me. I looked away to the next mannequin, who was already turning at the bottom of the stairs. The dress was coffee brown, and she wore it with a necklace of fat pearls.

"Too tomboy," I heard someone murmur.

The latecomer folded his arms and leaned back, as if he were going to sleep.

I was inattentive for the rest of the hour. By then it seemed to me that all Paris—including Americans and possibly people from Argentina—had joined in a cabal to make me look foolish. When I stood up in my agony of self-consciousness, I had marked four numbers on the chit—the numbers of the dresses I would come back to see next morning. The manufacturing woman—I had figured out this much about her—managed to take my slip and read it before handing it to the unsmiling salesgirl. Poor me. I didn't know then that every buyer is mad to see what every other one is doing. To me it only meant that the Parisians could start laughing at the Ohio girl even before she bought anything. I regretted making those marks all the more as I already knew it was the white shantung I would be taking back to Columbus (and fighting Mrs. Vincent Jones for).

The young man next to me had gotten up and was standing beside the row. When I got up, he politely said, *"Mam'selle,"* and he gestured for me to go ahead of him. I did so, because

I didn't know how to get around it. He walked beside me. As we passed the staircase, I partly expected Mlle Chanel to be looking down at us. Of course she wasn't there. It occurred to me there might not be a cabal to make me look foolish after all. In that case what did this man want?

VIII

THE PEOPLE were talking loudly now, and gathering their belongings up, or looking over their slips and yelling numbers back and forth.

I knew that at Chanel openings the door was barred till the end so you could not leave, but now that it was over, the Chanel people had all vanished as if they didn't care how we got out, and perhaps that accounts for the noise and yelling of the milling audience.

My companion walking discreetly beside me was getting terribly on my nerves. It was like having to drag someone else's suitcase around.

An old lady backed into him while she struggled to get her fur piece from under the chair legs, and then, exclaiming, she dropped her purse, too. He stepped back and helped her.

"*Oh, monsieur,*" she said, "*vous êtes gentil!*"

"*Oui, madame.* It's all right," he said, laughing.

"Isn't he nice," she said to me. "Isn't he nice to speak

English. I mean," she said, *"n'est-il pas gentil de parler anglais!"*
"Yes, he is," I said, but I was completely confused.

Mabel Normand was on the pavement at the bottom of the
steps, facing us as we came out into the sunlight.
"Why don't you come with me to the Crillon?" she said.
"We'll have an *apéritif* and talk things over. You can bring
Mr. . . ."
"De Gainsbourg," said my companion. "I represent the fab-
ric company."
"Oh, is that so! You speak English so well. I'm Daphne
Twomey of Weinburg's, Inc. Why don't you both come?" she
said, turning back to me.
The setting sun was right in my eyes and it glittered off the
black plume that crossed diagonally over the top of her hat.
Her powder was too thick on her face. It looked like rubber
coating.
"I have someplace else I have to go right now."
"Well, I'm going to talk to you eventually," she replied.
"Nice meeting you," she said to de Gainsbourg and walked
away.
"Want to go for a drink at the Ritz? It's by here," he said
as we stepped down to the pavement. "Or— I'm sorry, were
you in fact engaged? How rude of me!"
"No. I was just saying that. Just kidding her."
I had to chuckle along with him then, and after that I didn't
see how to break away, so we started to walk. In a few steps
we reached the Ritz. He stepped aside to point me toward the
open door and we went in together.
We took a small table and he asked me if it was all right.
Of course it was—it was very pretty and comforting. Better
than anything they had in Columbus. I looked at him while

he smiled at me. He wasn't fat, exactly. He was heavyish but in a handsome way.

"Am I all right?" he said, looking down at his suit.

I said "Yes," but tried not to put too much into it.

"Good. Excuse me, could I know your name, *mam'selle*?"

I told him.

"Ah, Louise. A French name for an American. It's such a beautiful French name, too."

"It isn't a French name. I just don't think it is."

"I think so," he said with a polite little nod. "But maybe I don't know." He looked happy and offered me a cigarette. "My name is Charles, anyway, even though you don't care."

I went so far as to take it but got out my own matches. He was ahead of me, though, with his lighter—a great big Ronson!

"It's very nice of you to come out with me. I thought you looked so—pretty—in the showroom. Please excuse me. Would you like tea or a drink? I think he's coming."

I was surprised he wasn't more anxious to make me forget the showroom and whatever it was that happened in there.

"Do you want something to eat instead? You can get food here, too."

"I'll just have tea, please," I told him, and he ordered away in French to the waiter, perhaps, as I thought, ordering tea with sleeping pills in it.

I sat back in my chair feeling faint from the powerful cigarette, while he glanced around the room.

"I'm so afraid that woman might have followed us here," he said in a low voice. "She seemed to like you very much."

"I never saw her before today. I don't know what she wants to talk about."

He made a face. "She probably just wants to take you to

the YMCA with her and give you a lunch of potato soup. Did you like the clothes?"

"Of course."

"Good. Chanel is good. Personally I am glad it's over."

"Are you a buyer from someplace in Paris?"

"No, I just come to the showings for my father's sake. He makes some of the fabrics they use. A gesture of politeness."

When I asked him why, he threw up his hands. He told me it bothers the couturiers that the fabric companies sell cloth to the copiers. But the couturiers can't do anything about it since they always owe the fabric companies money.

"So I came in for my father to pay his respects to the new clothes," he said, and shrugged his shoulders. "It's an offensive part of my job, but . . ." He shrugged again and started fussing around the spoons and teapots the waiter was bringing. "But it is so boring. Like today." He leaned forward. "When I sat down I thought, 'Oh, I can't stand this,' so out of boredom I pretended to draw little pictures of the clothes—which is a crime—and that is why they give you such a small bit of paper. I made three marks with my pencil, and—tak!—here comes the woman to confiscate my one-inch piece of paper. Oh, you like that story?" he exclaimed. "Now I understand you."

"Your father might be better off if you stayed home," I told him.

"Oh, well, maybe."

He pronounced it may-BE. The vision I'd had of Mlle Chanel conspiring with him to make me look foolish vanished forever, and a new picture formed in my mind, of her calling the police and having him taken to jail. He was beginning to seem sort of charming. His heavy, straight hair came down into his face as he looked at me, and he pushed it back. I wanted to make amends and I said, "So, this is a pretty bar."

"Why don't you call me Charles?" he said, leaning a little forward. "Don't look surprised."

"You know who I'm talking to," I told him.

"Yes, that's true." He thought a moment and said, "If I go over there, you could call me Charles. 'Charles, come back to the table!' "

"Sharl! Come back to the table."

"Ah, thank you, *mam'selle*," he said as we laughed.

"There was a man named Charles on the boat I came over on."

"Oh yes? I suppose so," he replied sadly.

"You don't have to burst into tears, you know," I said.

"No," he agreed, and appeared to forget about it, but still stared at me. Then the waiter came back. He offered me more tea but I declined it. When he had gone I mentioned the invitation I had had for dinner with the great couturier. I took M. Danon's note out of my purse, but I couldn't make head or tail of it. I was invited to join Florence————, avenue Victor-Hugo, for dinner. I had never heard of her. I didn't want to go, especially as it was already six-thirty by my watch. I laid the message on the table and stared at it a moment, trying to decide.

"I'm really too tired, and I don't know who she is. She may want me to buy something."

He reached over and took it off the white plate and read it carefully.

"Have you heard of her?" I asked. "Is she well known?"

"I never heard of her. Never. Let me call her for you, Louise. There is a phone number here, and I will ask her what she wants. She can't expect you to spend your evenings doing business with her. Shall I call her for you? Permit me!"

I took a cigarette out of my bag, and he instantly presented the lighter that was so like Harry's. It made me miss my ship friends.

"Don't worry so much," he said.

I nodded and he went away to the phone. When he returned he said, "You didn't call me, but I came back. And you don't have to go and see her."

He looked at me, sort of amused, and took up his drink. "She's a lovely little woman who is a dressmaker. She's a friend of Hattie."

"Hattie!"

"Yes. A friend of Hattie. Hattie told her you were coming to Paris. Hattie is worried about you, because you are only a girl of nineteen years, all alone in a great city"—he waved his arm around—"and though you may seem brave, so shy."

"I'm not shy."

"No? Well, maybe. She feels you are too shy to visit her, but I explained that you are tired tonight. She replied, 'And who are you, *monsieur?*' So, I told her we had met at Chanel, and she was glad you had that chance. To see Chanel, I mean. Not to meet me.

"She hopes you will come tomorrow evening and describe everything to her. She wants you to get a good sleep tonight, early to your hotel. She told me three times, and I promised."

"I wish you had put me on," I said after an agitated moment of smoking. It was painful for me to hear him say "Hattie" to me in that familiar way. Fortunately he didn't say it very well.

"I could not have believed you were only nineteen," he said after a moment.

"Why? How old are you?" I said meanly.

"Twenty-five. I think! I thought you were older than me, perhaps," he went on happily. "Though in France we don't think about the ages of men and women very much, as I know in America, the man must be three years older than the woman.

Here, we come together for love alone. Ho, she thinks I'm mad."

"We only met an hour ago, you know."

"Louise," he said carefully, "I know we just met, though it was three hours ago that I made a disturbance in there and you looked at me like this. . . ."

"I didn't look at you."

"Well, in spite of these things, would you come and have dinner with me? You see, I know it's terrible, but I have to meet my brother and his friend who are just home tonight from their military service. I can take you to your hotel, but then you might be all alone during the evening. It's not right for your first night in Paris."

I shook my head emphatically. But what would Hattie have done? I remembered all those people named Bill she'd gone to the Ritz Bar with. The RITZ BAR!

"Are we in the Ritz Bar?"

He nodded hard, as if to show he was ready to discuss any subject. "Nice, isn't it?" He was beginning to look so handsome and friendly to me, even if a bit too confident.

"Frankly," he said, "I don't think Hattie would want you to be alone after a hard day of work."

"You don't even know who Hattie is."

"No. But I know she's your auntie."

"Well, she doesn't know you from Adam." But all that kind of remark was in vain. He was exactly right about what Hattie would say.

We walked out a different door and emerged on the place Vendôme, which I had seen earlier that day. It was a traffic ring with a statue in the middle and a long, old building in two half-circles running around the edge. When the sky above it is pink and the traffic thin, as it was that evening, it really looks like some kind of playground. But then all cities look

127

like playgrounds to the foreigner. And then if you move there, you spend your time hurrying and planning just like everybody else does, and you don't look at anything and it's not like a playground anymore.

We walked along without talking to each other; perhaps he was embarrassed, as I was. It's all very well to say you'll go somewhere with someone you've just met, but once you start to act it out, you can't help thinking: "Now he thinks you have nothing better to do than walk around with him" or "He's probably stupid" and so on. Besides, he can't take your arm yet, and so you zigzag to keep from touching him. You can't look up at him as you go because he is now taller and it would be too much like what Betty and I used to call "a kissing situation." So then if you do hit him, you are forced to pretend you didn't realize it, and he thinks maybe you can't walk a straight line for medical reasons. I don't remember any thoughts like these troubling my walks alongside Harry, but of course I was trying to get *away* from him. And most of the time, it seems to me, I stared as hard as I pleased at my friend Wentworth. My mother used to say you always know the right man when he comes—he's the one who makes you feel bad for no reason.

The air was humid and the sky was still light, but the streetlights were on. It was the blue hour. We turned off the rue de la Paix, Charles just touching my elbow. A cat inside a shop watched us approach, then ran up onto the counter, where a woman swatted at him. What was she doing to those small pastries at this hour, the blue hour? I always feel there is such an aura of peculiarity to life in Paris, I never can believe it's real and not a play, and yet I have spent so much time there over the course of my life that I should be used to it. But since I am always thinking "Here I am in Paris" the whole time, perhaps I assume the Parisians are thinking it, too, and really longing to go out and sight-see while they know they must stay in the shop and look "workaday."

Next I remember emerging at the place de l'Opéra opposite the beautiful building itself. But I looked at it only out of my left eye, because it is so remarkable I knew if I really looked I'd have to say something and I didn't want to give way. And for all he knew, we had buildings like that all over Columbus.

He said, "Are you tired? We can go slower, or get a cab."

"No, I'm fine."

"Or I can carry you. Of course I was just kidding. Louise, I must prepare you for our dinner conversation with my brother and his friend. First, you must decide whether you are in favor of the Masons, and if you support the Communists or the Croix de Feu. And, remember, in France now we have the thing called the Popular Front, and when you hear those words, 'Front Populaire,' you must get angry and hit the table—like this."

He made a fist and showed it to me, then resumed his cheerful talking.

"Are you tired? We are almost at the restaurant. Ah, I'm so pleased you decided to come. It will be a great treat for these two boys. They have been in the army now for six months. In Nîmes, that's in the South of France. It is very hard for them to adjust to such a small town."

"Oh, were they drafted?"

He turned right around and faced me, and I thought for a moment he was going to yell angrily, "Yes, they were drafted!" But he was just holding open the door.

This was not the small romantic place I had expected, but more like Chock Full O'Nuts. Tourists don't visit such restaurants, but as far as I'm concerned, they are always good.

The atmosphere is right, unless of course you'd rather be in a dark place on horrible fat cushions that make you feel that you are sitting in a harem.

"We like this place," said Charles. "Not very elegant, though."

"Well, I like it."

"Ah," said Charles. "That's good. There's my friend, Georges. He says they are over there."

Charles saluted a sweating dark man, who was balancing a tray piled with enough plates for forty or so people, and the man saluted in return. Charles put his arm around me, and we walked down to the back, under a row of big lamps, to the red banquette at the end of the room. Two almost-bald young men sat side by side and stared at us. But before we had gotten very close they both jumped up and gave me a series of nods that were almost bows, and these bows turned into efforts to pull chairs out for me.

Charles clapped one on the shoulder and shook the other's hand over the table, meanwhile laughing and talking, of course in French, all their voices raised. This only took a bare instant and then Charles said, "Louise, *je vous présente*, I present you my brother Philippe de Gainsbourg, and François Foyot, two fighting men of France." I shook hands. They both looked so open-faced as they smiled and welcomed me.

They looked alike—brown eyes and almost no hair. I couldn't remember which one was Charles's brother. For my own sake I wasn't curious, as neither one was anything like him. We sat down opposite, and the three men all talked at once—too fast for me to understand any part of it. But when I looked up from my purse, cigarette in hand, there were cigarette lighters everywhere, and those two were saying *"mademoiselle!"* in demanding voices.

A waiter came and we all ordered *bifteks* from him, along with some other things that were out of my hands.

As I smoked and began to relax, I heard them discussing Lelong. Charles said something, then quickly turned to me: "It is Lucien Lelong. We are wondering what he will do."

I nodded.

"And how is La Légitime?" one of the strangers asked.

"La Légitime is our mother," reported Charles to me.

"She is an exquisite woman," said the other, speaking English with difficulty. "Her . . ."

"Underwear . . ."

"Her underwear is made by nuns in Mexico. The nuns *sew* her underwear," he said, "like this," and he made the motions of sewing and squinting.

We all laughed. The waiter brought Charles and me glasses of Dubonnet we had not asked for. Charles laid his arm along the back of my chair. One of the soldiers saw, and suddenly said "*Mademoiselle!* What has four pairs of pants and lives in Philadelphia?"

"How did you all learn English?" I said crankily.

"We spent our summers in Mentone," said Charles. "There is a great English population there, so we had many English playmates."

"*Ce sont des fils à papa, mademoiselle,*" said their friend. "*La jeunesse d'orée!* They don't work like you and me must work."

Charles smiled cynically at him. "Poverty has kept this boy's mind from developing. He's below the monkey stage. But it's not his fault."

"Ah, no," said the friend. "It's the government's fault."

I braced myself, thinking they might be about to pound the table, but instead the friend said, "Look at Charles. His courage tonight at this table. And, yet, he is a man without a car! He has no car."

"I crashed my car. Into a Dubonnet truck."

"A six-wheel," added Philippe.

131

"And each wheel rolled over my poor car, until it looks like a little . . . tambourine."

François winked at me. "The father will buy him a new one. A bigger one! The father is a Mason, *mademoiselle.*"

The two others sighed.

"Mademoiselle," continued the friend, "Mees! Do you know it is against the law to own a cigarette lighter in Yugoslavia?"

Then he turned and went on about something to the other two. The waiter came with our plates, and I tried to eat and put all of them out of my mind. I felt I must be dreaming— as if the potatoes on my plate were joke potatoes. I didn't fight the feeling, either, since I was only here on business.

The two brothers were shaking their heads. Charles looked sideways at me and chuckled, then shook his head some more.

"You see, Louise," he said, gesturing casually with his fork, "François is a Communist."

François flung his arms up in the air in annoyance. "Listen. This government tells us we cannot help the . . ."

He turned to Philippe, and Philippe said wearily, "The rebels in Spain."

"The rebels in Spain. Nonintervention. All the time, the factories in France are selling weapons to Franco. As much as he wants! Where will we be if Franco wins the war?" He held three fingers up in front of my face and counted one by one. "Germany, Italy, and Spain. All around France."

"Let's talk about something for Louise," said Philippe.

"Pourquoi?" exclaimed François, laughing. "Louise! Do you . . ." He broke off and whispered with Charles's brother, who rolled his eyes, then cleared his throat.

"This . . . fool wants to know, do you enjoy voting?"

Now they all looked curiously while I chewed away at my steak. "Oh, I love it," I told them.

"Ça suffit, François," Philippe said, as François began once

again to wave his arms around. "Let's go somewhere to dance. Louise wants to dance."

"I don't think so," Charles interposed. "Though," he said, turning to me, "it can be fun in some of these places."

"What a damage the Ballier is closed," François muttered.

"Not a damage, a *pity*."

"*Oh là!* You see, *mademoiselle*—I have not been to Mentone and I am *ridicule!*"

"How about the Tabarin? It's good and crowded and it might be rather fun."

"You have never been there, Philippe," said Charles.

"No, it's true. But I have been to Zelli's!"

"We will go to Zelli's."

"There's no dancing there," said Charles.

"Ah, no—only nude women who come and talk to you!" François laughed, producing agony in the other two.

I said I'd rather go back and go to bed. Philippe and François, so lively before, turned suddenly into a pair of quiet, humble boys, as if they'd had no right to expect me to go dance with them. But their spirits came back when our black coffee arrived and I asked the waiter to bring some milk. The two soldiers laughed at me and cried "Good morning!" while Charles shook his head at them. I laughed, but I didn't know of course that in France only babies drink *café au lait* after 11:00 A.M.

We left them in front of the restaurant, bowing repeatedly, and then Philippe took hold of Charles's buttonhole and appeared to give him a little lecture on how to go around with women. François Foyot enjoyed it very much.

They lit their cigarettes—free Gauloises from the army— and walked away rapidly, in a hurry to dance. I went to the curb in hopes Charles would tell me how to go about getting to my hotel, and from there we watched their progress. When they came to a streetlamp, they would turn back to us to wave their arms and yell, *"Adieu, mademoiselle. Adieu, Sharl."* They did this at least five times. Once François made punching motions and instead of *adieu* cried, "Joe Louis!"

When we got into the cab, Charles asked me if I was going to Patou the next day, and I said I was and wondered if I was to take it for granted he was going, too. Does he expect to spend every day with me—days and days together? I wondered in my stupid ignorance. Days and days. Who does he think he is?

In the cab I sat with my fists between my knees. He was watching my profile while the lights came and went. It was intolerable. I turned so all he could see was my hair. And that is how I threw away those minutes in the cab, while Charles guarded my hat.

The cab brought us up to the hotel door. I was about to say "Good-bye" and just bolt, but Charles got out and grabbed my hand as I went by him.

"Sleep well, Louise," he said. I nodded and ran in. I mean that I nodded the way you nod when someone puts their head in the door of the subway car and says, "Is this the Broadway local?"

I did sleep well. I would have overslept, but the inquisitive woman came in with the several pitchers again and made me coffee at my bedside. She not only pursed her lips, but this morning shook her head at nothing. I supposed she must fit somewhere into the conspiracy to make me look stupid, and the proof was the way she banged the shutters hard against the wall. I pictured the night porter telling her, "Muggsie brought her in. It was mighty late, too," then winking.

I WENT BACK to Chanel that morning to make my choices, but could hardly believe I was in the same place. The dresses lay in heaps all around, and there was the racket of the buyers yelling in all languages with their salesgirls. I bought the one dress I needed to buy to keep the invitation open, and the dress I bought was number one, and I happened to buy it in my size.

Hattie had not directed me in this, so I reasoned that I had no choice but to buy something for all those over-five-foot-nine-inch Columbus women. I even told the salesgirl I didn't like to see those tall girls overlooked.

I paid with one of the Lazarus documents I had brought with me, sitting down on a little gold straight chair to do the signing, while my Pinkerton went away to make arrangements to have the dress sent. I looked up to see Daphne Twomey at my side, only this time covered with an appalling piece of fur—almost head to foot, and with no expense spared to make it look sort of plaid.

"I just heard about Willi Hanke," she told me, bending down. "I don't know about you, but I have no sympathy for people who do that kind of thing."

I'd never heard of him, so I didn't have any sympathy either. I went back to my bank order and she sat down next to me.

"What did you buy?"

"I bought one dress."

"How many and which one? The brown middy dress? It's a mistake."

"Say, who's Willi Hanke?" I said, and I smiled in an encouraging manner.

"A German. A German from the Argentine, if you can beat that. Hanke was a very big buyer. He killed himself last night. Oh, it's a long, long story. I saw it coming in 1930, when he gave a party at Maxim's, his *first* year in Paris, you understand, and invited all the members of the Gin Club and expected them to come! Of course they were there anyway because they go to Maxim's every night! Willi Hanke slinks in incognito. . . . What do you think he was dressed as? Just guess. As a woman. People forget that we are here as businessmen and -women, not to get on first-name terms with the cream of the elite or whatever. We aren't here to make friends at all. But Willi Hanke! He *never* knew where to draw the line. I've seen him where he had rouge on in public. Oh, I've seen too much of it."

When this pause came, I looked up and assumed a disbelieving expression. "I just can't imagine that," I told her, and really, it is hard to picture, but I wasn't thinking about it; in fact, her story was the last thing on my mind.

"I'll tell you the rest over lunch."

I began to lie. I told her I had a meeting at my hotel in ten minutes. And after the meeting? A conference.

"Honey," she said eerily, "are you in a jam?"

"Me?" I said. "I'm not in a jam!" And then I laughed a careless laugh to prove it. I got up and went quickly toward the door, but she was right behind. Her manners were so awful and unpleasant that I was determined not to *look* at her; in my mind she took strange shapes. She widened and got slower but more narrow-minded, like a big radio on wheels with a mind of its own, not caring if it rolled over dirt or parquet, so long as it could get hold of someone and tell them the boring things that came into its mind. I waved for a cab and saw that she had put her hand up, too. When it came she said, "I'll drop you."

I gave the name of my hotel to the driver, and she said to him, "Stop at the Crillon first." She sat back into her corner to look at me better, or so it seemed, and her fur sat up around her rubberish face.

I kept my eyes on the driver's neck. How kind he seemed.

But Daphne started talking again after a few seconds—first just snorting a few times. Perhaps she wanted me to ask "What is it, Miss Twomey?" "Well!" she said. "It beats me what Fred Lazarus is up to. Does he have some of his other people over here? Is that who you're meeting?"

"I guess Willi Hanke had a lot of troubles, all right," I remarked.

"Oh, him! He wasn't worth the powder to blow him to hell. What kind of man shoots himself in the head? Say, you look like you forgot that one dress of yours. Was it too heavy to carry?"

"I had them send it to the hotel."

"Driver," said Daphne, jumping up, "never mind the Crillon. I'll be going on with *mademoiselle*."

"Crillon?" said the driver.

"No, never mind it. No Crillon. Keep going till I tell you!

"Fifteen years ago today *I* was riding down to the Hudson

River piers to count the number of short skirts and cloche hats on the women coming home," said my companion. "I did it for my boss. Or he sent me over to the Stock Exchange to count the pairs of tan shoes on the men, as opposed to black. That was my job and I was mighty glad to have it. That was my apprenticeship.

"In those days they didn't take a little snip off the street and ask her how she'd like to go to Paris for a week! And I never heard of such a thing."

I had kept up my communion with the driver's neck. She was shifting around on her part of the seat, and making believe my hat was in her way. I turned and she handed it to me, saying, "You a college girl?"

"Nope."

"Well, maybe your last name is Lazarus, for all I know."

"No, it isn't! Hattie Merrill hired me."

"Oh, I remember Hattie Merrill."

She spoke so indifferently that I couldn't believe she did. Imagine the two of them together: Hattie in one of her tilted "saucer" hats and smiling face, and Daphne Twomey towering above her like a giant big Beefeater!

We pulled up to the hotel, so there was no need to hear Daphne theorize on Hattie's secret problems, or what awful things she had "seen coming" about her. I went through my purse for the right bill. What would this go-by-ground say if I tried paying by Jean's system right in front of her? I was getting beyond that anyway. I knew that francs and centimes were different colors.

While I waited for my change—poised to jump out—she thought of a few more things she wanted to say, and she said them in a mean voice.

"You'll never get anywhere in retailing unless you learn to get along with people. Bend a little. It's a small world and everybody needs the other fellow. But the most important thing of all is, you only get out of it what you put into it."

I was making my way out backward as she uttered these words. I had to look right into her eyes to understand her. She was looking at me, too, from her corner, but not in any particular way. She looked, exactly, as she might have looked if the taxi had had a trapdoor in the roof and a bunch of pelts had been dropped through it on her head.

But abruptly she looked past me and her face lit up. I slammed the cab door and turned to see my friend Charles, leaning beside the brass doors of the hotel and balancing a bicycle with one foot.

"Well, look who's here!" said Daphne, but the cab took her away.

Charles smiled and came forward to where I stood, leaving the bike where it was. The sun was on his face and he squinted affectionately at me. I was completely unprepared.

"Please excuse me. I thought that you might like to go and have lunch with me before you have to go to Patou. Was that big Dempsey-Tunney? She fits her name! Louise, you look tired."

"Well, I don't get what you're talking about. Wait a minute."

I hurried past him and walked as fast as I could through the lobby. Once inside my room I threw off my hat and got under the covers. The shutters were closed at this time of day, and the faint little bars of light—as faint and blurry as the street sounds now were—comforted me. It came over me that I was in Paris, that place I'd been seeing where the people and the buildings were all so odd. That little cat, for example! I could go back down the street and find it, and buy it a pound of suet and watch it eat because I was here, too. Oh, Paris, City of Light, I thought, where probably every light meant a broken heart. And yet mine wasn't one of them.

I jumped up and took a shower, and then I put on my white dress, my tennis dress. I wished to heck at that moment that I might find Jean and Ed when I went downstairs. As for missing anyone else, if I hadn't seen them in the past week, they were so remote I couldn't remember them.

As I made up to look like Hedy, I couldn't help thinking of when Jean and I chased Wentworth and made him leave his conversation, and the suggestive remarks I must have seemed to make in front of that person in the closet. I actually trembled at that shameful memory. And now there was a French *monsieur* downstairs. Was he really fat, or just heavy in a manly, attractive way? I hadn't really dared to look at him yet.

I left my purse behind, just putting my money and my bank order in my pocket, along with a letter I found on the chiffonier. In the hall the curious maid went by me, fixing her eyes on my shoes, for some reason. Yet the shoes I wore with my white dress were very tame. A man could practically have worn them!

I managed to rejoin Charles without looking him in the face. Since he had his bicycle, we had to walk. It wasn't hot at all, and the sky was exactly the color of morning glories, the favorite flower of every lady in Columbus, Ohio. The air was not only clear, it was soft and fragrant, like something a hostess would want to pump into her living room before a party. New York can't compare with Paris in these departments!

It was only eleven, and Charles said we had plenty of time to go down by the river, which was the "beating heart of Paris." We turned down the rue de Marignan the other way and came out on a square. At the end of it, you could see a gray wall and tall trees, with no buildings or trees visible beyond them—nothing but the morning-glory sky. I got so I couldn't help looking all around me, though I still walked as though I were walking alone.

In front of the wall, there were bookstalls, and in front of them, strips of lawn with children running around screaming.

My excitement grew to the point that I had to look at Charles—at least his arms as they pushed the bike. His sleeves were rolled and his arms were tanned. He had a jacket, but it was thrown over the handlebars.

I couldn't look up at his face. This was no different from the time I'd spoken to a man dressed up as Buster Brown! I'd sat beside him trembling, and kept my eyes fixed on my mother. Answers to the questions he asked me I addressed to her. I'd told her my name and the name of my school.

"Sorry to have this bicycle today, Louise," said Charles, "but I had to do some things this morning. You know I ruined my car. But I love this bicycle," he exclaimed suddenly, and lifted it up for me to see. "See, it's an Humber, the greatest English bicycle! Those people are *mad* for sport. There are no French bicycles like this one. I would love to import them someday. I would make a huge fortune."

"Could you leave the business you're in?"

"I pray so every day. Ah, I would bring so much happiness to France, if the people would only try the Humber. I would be rich and loved. A gift of *joie* for the large and the small people of my country! Do you have to be rich to own an Humber? Shame! Of course not! Rich and poor meet as equal on their Humbers."

"Bet *I* couldn't afford one."

"Maybe I would actually give you one."

Sure, I thought.

"Wait a moment, Louise."

He left me standing in the path, near enough to the wall to see over it and onto the smooth blue river. The sunlight hit each small wave separately, making a view that was happy and pretty, and it had nothing to do with buildings, history, or retailing. What had we walked into? The air was soft; the children were yelling hard. I just wanted to throw off my old self.

I went to the wall and placed my hands on the curving stone that capped it. I leaned over. Down below—too far to jump—there was a cobblestone walk at the water level. There were hunched men fishing there every few yards, as far as you could see in both directions, looking like blots in the glare of the river. Why should they have been wearing coats in that weather? But perhaps it was no sillier than that Daphne and half the other fashion connoisseurs should be lugging their minks around.

Just below where I stood was a pointed little boat, with no paint on it, and nobody in it. Why shouldn't I get in, since it was all clean and ready, and since I hadn't ever yet been in a boat?

Charles came up behind me and I jumped. Somehow I had jumped into him. He put one arm around me and kissed me on the cheek, then put a silly-looking waffle into my hands and told me to eat it. Then he stretched himself and leaned against the wall—smiling but not too confident. I turned right around and tried to blind my eyes by staring at the river.

"Ah, it's so stupid that you have to go to this Patou show!" he said in a moment. "I feel like we are in school."

"Is Patou by the river?"

"It's place Vendôme," he said sadly. "So stupid—over by the Ritz again."

"I wish I could stay here. I'd like to get into that boat down there."

"You know," he said calmly, "maybe you should give up your job."

I said I might, and we started walking again. Privately I was thinking that quitting my job was a good idea. I could hardly have said what my job even was. I still couldn't look at him, but I was ready to give up my job right then.

I was so struck by the appearance of the sunlight on everybody's newly washed hair. That included Charles's—especially a sun-bleached part that fell down in front and made him have to toss his head while he talked, and then again every time he happened to turn and look down at me.

We stopped at a newspaper stand, and he offered to get me a copy of French *Vogue*. I realized then how far outside the world of couture and all that he was. He was just trying to please me.

I shook my head. "Hey, Sharl," I began, "do you know who Willi Hanke is?"

"No," he said, "I never heard of him."

"He killed himself."

"Ah. He probably had a reason."

"Probably. He was a famous buyer from the Argentine."

"*Oh là.*"

"He probably bought too much and was afraid to go back home!"

"Maybe he had doubts about his own good taste. Want to go to a café, Louise? You need more for your lunch than one *galette*. It's really for dessert, anyway."

But I wouldn't leave the riverbank, which was more and more filled with children and their hoops and balloons. They ignored the book and newspaper sellers, and the book and newspaper sellers ignored them. All, as I said, had freshly washed hair and little white shirts and dresses, and happy, intent faces. Half the time they were screaming with indignation. It infected me and I didn't want to go anywhere else.

We went along with the river on our right hand, and he

just watched me look around. I'd say, "Maybe I *will* just quit, anyway," anytime I saw something that pleased me, which was all the time. A tall bridge came into view, with what looked like stone birds all along it, stretching their wings.

"What's it going to do, fly up?"

"Do bridges fly in America?"

"We don't usually put wings on them over there," I said with a little bit of scorn.

"I see. Well, one day, who knows? Paris will wake up and the bridge will have flown away. Perhaps to Juan-les-Pins. The Masons will blame the Jews! The Catholics will blame the Masons! It will be the end of the Front Populaire, once and for all. Then Hitler will come, to pacify us."

"Hitler!" I said with scorn. I put my finger under my nose and raised my right arm.

He laughed, probably out of pity. "You know," he said, "my grandfather wants to fight him in a duel. But the Führer refuses. Such a coward! My grandfather is funny, Louise. He isn't worried. You see, he fought a duel once, in the Parc-des-Princes. That is where the great duels are always fought— over there, on the west side of Paris. And yet he wasn't really rich enough to fight a duel there. But he did it! Now in the case of Hitler, he says, fair play is out of the question. Not necessary. He says he will arrange to put only a little powder in the guns. Hitler shoots. Actually, the ball falls out on the ground, but Hitler doesn't see it. At that moment my grandfather touches his ear—ow!—but says bravely, 'It is nothing.' Discouraged but proud of himself, Hitler turns around to go home. My grandfather pulls out his tiny pistol and shoots him dead in the back."

"I doubt if they'd let him load the guns!"

Charles shook his head. "I told him so, and do you know what he said? 'Perhaps I can shoot Pétain.' "

"He sounds just like my father. My father is mad all the time."

"Oh yes? Who does he want to shoot at?"

Here we reached the edge of the place de la Concorde and started across it, Charles taking my arm. I tried hard to remember the guy's name. It *had* been Roosevelt. We entered the Tuileries and it came to me.

"He wants to shoot Edmund Wilson."

"Why? Who is that?"

I shrugged, thinking how unlikely it was that my father had a reason. "He's probably a Commie, I guess."

" 'Sharl,' " said Charles.

So I said, "He's probably a Commie, Sharl, old boy."

We crossed the gardens, making our way to the rue de Rivoli, which I could see through the trees and where we would find a place to eat. I was thinking a bit dejectedly that he was less likely to give me another kiss once we got out there. He was telling me about his nighttime trip to London in a plane—how red sparks burst out into the air. The stewardess sat down beside him and talked all about her boyfriend, which made him long to be on the ground again for some reason.

We left the cool park and crossed up to a big café that had tables outdoors. Charles hung his bicycle on the back of a chair and then made me sit on it, so he could watch us both at the same time. We had *saucisses frites*, and while we ate, he whistled "Every Little Breeze Seems to Whisper Louise."

Our beers were brought to us, foaming out of the tops of tall "Tonique" glasses. I drank half mine down, and then I stretched out to get my legs into the sun. I was facing the street and I watched many long black cars—some with the tops down, and one with only a dog for a passenger. All of them resembled Mr. Lazarus's big car, which Hattie used for errands now and then, and sometimes came home in. If only she would get in it and be transported over here, I mused. And then she could pull up to this curb, jump out and fix her hat and laugh. "Just a minute, dear, I'm all blowsy." Then she'd say, "And here's Red!"—and Red would jump out and climb on me, and then on all the Parisians.

I opened one eye. Charles was looking my way, but it may have been at the bicycle. He went back to his singing.

"Oh, Lord."

"Well, you look so *mignonne*. I can't help it."

"No, I don't."

"Yes, you do. Not like these women that are everywhere."

I looked at them, but only long enough to see a bunch of hats. "Never compare women," I told him. "Each is nice in her own way."

He raised his eyebrows in surprise. I asked him if he had seen Daphne's fur coat.

"No, not today! That woman is mad. You see, Louise, a woman like that needs a husband, and feels cold. But the cold is inside. Only a husband can help her."

He said all this to me in a reasoning voice. My mother had told me the same thing plenty of times.

"You know what she needs?" I said. "She needs a strait-jacket. And I bet she'll be there, chasing me around this afternoon."

"I'm going," he said. "I hope to get her in a duel, maybe."

How different this show was from Chanel. We arrived late, but it was like a wild party and no one noticed us. Patou served champagne. He encouraged everybody to talk and smoke, and the salesgirls didn't even appear till the end. I remember that mine said happily to me, "Miss Anna Gould buys all her dresses here! She *was* married to Boni de Castellane. Ah! He was in here every day."

The room had windows all down one side, and the air was smoky enough that objects at the other end appeared a mile or so away. All were waving their bracelets around while the dresses came and went—sometimes four at a time. You couldn't concentrate any more than if you were at a circus. And yet I could see how this approach might also work.

Charles and I stood gazing, leaning our heads against the striped gray silk that covered the wall. I hadn't seen anything like this before—a huge mob of dressy, important men and women, all shoveled in together. In my experience such people went around alone, and even put up curtains in their car windows.

Patou was making sophisticated, austere suits around that time, and those are what I remember. I also liked the very slender high heels the mannequins had on, and I vowed I'd get some. I made a tremendous effort to memorize two numbers for later, and eventually I sent those models home: number eleven, for a purple afternoon dress with a white embroidered hanky in the pocket, and number twenty-eight for a tulle evening dress. It had a petal skirt that was sort of daffy—daffy enough for Hattie to fall in love with it and give it to me. In a few years I found a little flaw in the material of the underskirt and quickly gave it away.

The other thing that was going on that afternoon was that Charles was whispering in my ear. I didn't pay too much attention to him, having moved to that stage where I regarded him as totally my own.

The woman I had seen in the gray Schiaparelli suit the day before was here, too, circulating and shouting "Hey!" at every-body. The front of her suit came as a great shock to me. It had red lobster buttons! They were large for buttons, and were sewed on so that they appeared to be crawling up toward her neck. Above them was her soft, kind face—well, it was really an unfortunate choice, a certain kind of fashion mistake that often preoccupied Hattie. "Too much adventurism," she called it.

Charles had been wandering around while I made my arrangements, but as soon as I stood up he came to my side with a middle-aged man and introduced us. I don't remember who the man was. Never saw him again anyway. Why do I remember these things?

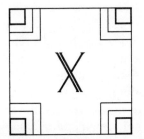

X

WHEN I PUT my little book of money orders back in my pocket, I found the letter. I decided to read it then and there, while Charles stood a few feet away, his hands in his pockets, still in conversation with the man. It was from Betty.

August 31

Dear Louise,

You've only been gone a few days but it seems like a dog's age. I sure do miss seeing you every day. There's nobody to talk to unless you count *Ellen Schutz*, but I don't count her. She's been acting so suspicious of me and I can't figure out why. I feel as if I must have done something shameful, but I haven't— at least not that *she'd* know about.

I guess she's just my cross to bear.

I guess you're thinking "I don't care about Betty Wheeler's little troubles when I'm over here in Paree." Well, I don't blame you! I hope you'll remember all the things you see, including people. Otherwise you won't be able to tell me about it.

149

I'd be just sick if I thought you weren't coming back.

Come back soon. My dad wants to meet you. Maybe he thinks you'll get married to him.

Always,
Betty

P.S. Your aunt is mailing this. She sure is nice.

I folded it up with care and returned it to my pocket. I was so awfully lucky, compared to my friend.

I went to Charles to tell him I had to leave. I had to go to the old lady's dinner. But because his friend was talking, I couldn't speak right away. Without turning, Charles put his arm around my back. His jacket smelled faintly of smoke. This was more delicious to me than the kiss.

Finally we said good-bye to the man and went out through the black and white tiled hall to the street so that I could get a cab. When I realized he had to wait for his bicycle to be brought, I waved away the cab and went in with him again. I wanted to stand with his arm on my back for a little while more.

While we stood together in the hall with the great men and women of fashion running around and shouting out names, and the concierge's apprentice, who was eighty years old, coming and going in search of the bicycle, I became quite spoiled. Why did I have to go every place I didn't want to go, and get talked to by old ladies? Hattie's friend seemed as dreary as an old cobweb.

We went slowly out again and down the steps behind a trio of men in gray suits. They kept stopping to turn to each other, or just jiggle their keys while they sought for the right word. Or they would nod and smile back at Charles, not grasping the situation. It was raining slightly and they didn't grasp that either. Perhaps they represented the Big Three of Paris: Galeries Lafayette, Au Printemps, and La Samaritaine. Perhaps they were from the Louvre, or maybe they were three famous generals. Slowly down they went, and once in the street, we found that their three long cars had kept the cabs at some distance.

"Masons!" murmured Charles. "Masons of the worst kind. Do they ever think of the poor working man with his bicycle?"

"Why don't you put that down, and ride to that old lady's, and tell her something happened to me?" I burst out.

"Are you so afraid of her?" he said, looking around in surprise. "I should never have said you would go to her house!"

"Tell her I saw some Masons and it upset me."

That made us laugh. Charles stopped walking, and I saw a woman swerve to go around him. As she did so, she looked back at me. It was Daphne Twomey, but she didn't stop.

"What if she herself is a Mason?" he went on. "A woman Mason? They say they are more dangerous than the men!"

I looked away from him, around the square—which is a poor name for something as special as this one was. Cabs were rushing out of it, down the rue de la Paix, but a sort of steam was rising from the street and they looked blurry. I had one of those feelings again, like I'd had at noontime when I got under the covers of my bed.

"So this is Paris," I said to him.

"Yes, it is."

"When you just think of everybody over in Columbus," I said quickly, "it's hard to believe. I know you think I'm screwy," I said. "Could you get me that cab over there?"

We waved down this cab, though it had no windshield wipers—the very kind of thing my mother was always visualizing. I was too abashed to wait around for a better one, and I was wet besides.

Before closing the door Charles leaned in and said, "Louise,

I wish you would never go back to Columbus. I hope you *never* will."

I looked up into his eyes, which were so kind, and then the driver yelled something, and Charles chuckled and shut the door. I heard later the driver had said to him, "Why don't you get in and come along, too?" or something like that. But at the time I assumed they were laughing over whether I was too young, or whether I was homely.

We were in the rue de la Paix and it was *l'heure bleue* again. I had showed the driver the address, but I didn't care if we went there—that was the effect great happiness was having on me. Take this woman, for example. I was going to have trouble paying attention to anything she said! She was Hattie's friend, of course, but Hattie was friends with a lot of strange birds, and that was her own term.

The sky was still luminous, but the car headlights were on, and so were the lights in the small shops.

I sank down with my eyes closed. How did you say, "Cabbie, wait for me. I'll be right back." I wondered. Or, "Cabbie, I've got to shake hands with an old lady, then I'll come back out."

Finally I jabbed his shoulder. *"Attendez, s'il vous plaît!"*

He grunted in reply. I thought we had settled it. To crown this triumph, he turned onto the Champs-Élysées, and for the first time I could see the Arc de Triomphe sitting in splendor at the end of it, beautifully lit up and looking eternal at the top of the small rise.

"C'est beau, n'est-ce pas?" said the driver.

"Oui," I replied. *"Oui oui."*

Then he launched on a story that I couldn't understand at all. He was cheerful. He took his left hand off the wheel and moved it in small circles while he spoke. He was quite a bit like that cabdriver who'd ordered himself a wife from Italy. That man probably had six children by this time, supposing they had all been twins. He would name them all Fiorello. He could make all of them into organ grinders, wearing little pairs of white gloves.

The majesty of France seemed to be making me homesick. Well, maybe I was one of those saps who would rather be in a shack than a palace, provided it's home! Certainly the arch at the bottom of Fifth Avenue *was* a little like a shack, compared to this one.

We drove right at the arch with about twenty cars alongside us. It was terribly gigantic and grand. But at the last minute we went around and not underneath, as a small plane had recently done.

This woman lived out along the avenue Victor-Hugo in a slightly run-down building. I saw it through the rain on the windshield, and I didn't want to go in. If she was poor, how much worse the whole thing would be! If she was rich and full of life, I still didn't want to go in. People of nineteen really only want opportunities to flirt, and if they can't flirt, they want to be in their beds asleep, and that's why I felt this way. I also feared that dinner would be a big bowl of ox brains. This was a dish someone had put in front of my father once, in France during the First World War. He had never stopped warning me not to eat it. Its "mere appearance" had frightened him!

I climbed out and looked at the yellowish wall and the bluish door. I advanced toward it. There was faint odor of ox brains, even down on the street. I turned back and handed the driver a small bill, to keep his loyalty while I was inside. He touched his cap and drove away—getting smaller and smaller till he blended in with a mass of little red lights in the distance!

Except for these, the road wasn't lit. This wasn't the Champs-Élysées and it lacked the happy atmosphere around the river. It was more like a regular street somewhere. It must be "the real Paris." Just what I needed! What I didn't know was that I was near the site of Hattie's favorite part of Paris and the cause of her happiest memories, the Bois de Boulogne, where they'd made the horses gallop so fast and she'd screamed so much that she'd completely lost her voice, year after year. That had occurred a quarter mile from where I now stood, feeling so cranky and deprived.

I pulled the bell handle under a sign that read "Florence: Robes Modes Nouveautés." I knew what that meant—novelties. Circus costumes! I'd be eating my ox brains opposite a woman who made circus costumes!

The door flew open and there was an old lady, apparently on her knees. She rattled away in French and I let her drag me through the opening, my heel catching on the sill. We went across a stone paved yard, her pressure on my wrist sort of pulling me down to her height, which seemed to be about four feet. We went under an archway and through another door, then together we *raced* up a flight of stairs in the pitch-dark. She murmured, *"Venez, venez"* and "Come on, miss." She pounded on a door somewhere, then opened it herself and marched me into the hall, as if she were a federal marshal and I were the most deadly criminal in U.S. history.

When Hattie's friend came in, this woman pointed at me and uttered another stream of words I didn't understand. It might have been "She's a fighter, but I got her anyway." Florence laid a hand on my arm but otherwise ignored me and listened hard to the old woman, whose excitement was still building. Maybe she was a fashion scout, and she was upset by what I was wearing!

She came to the end and walked away down an unlit hall.

"Virginie is so happy to have a guest in the house from America," said Florence, leading me through another door. "Hattie used to like her very much. She said she was afraid

154

Virginie would jump up and hang by nothing one of these days."

I nodded. She knew Hattie, all right.

We were in a dark room crammed with furniture with only one light on at the far end. We went to it, side by side, and sat down in a pair of identical striped chairs, which were set close together, as if for a secret conversation.

"Did Hattie say I was going to invite you? Perhaps you didn't want to come and visit such an old person." She tilted her head as she said this, but I held out a while longer, just murmuring something confused.

"That's a pretty dress," she went on. *"Pour le sport?* For sports?"

"I guess it needs ironing," I replied, looking down at it.

"Linen always needs ironing," she said happily. "It's a both-ersome material, but you see, I like it, too," and she touched at the hem of her own dress, which was also linen but did not need any ironing. In fact it was a Hattie type of dress, having an oval neckline trimmed with eyelets and embroidery.

She was older than Hattie, though. Her hair was gray, and she wore it in a chignon. In spite of all this, she looked as summery and pleasant as a milkweed in that dark room full of old furniture. She just wasn't the ox-brain type, nor was she the circus-costume type either. If she did have a circus-costume business, she must have gotten someone else to run it, in some other part of town. We sat there in the lamplight like two princesses, and I was almost as serene as she was in spite of the alarm I'd gone through.

She folded her hands and said, "Now, who was that man I spoke to on the phone? I ask only because of Hattie, you know. I hope you don't mind. Ah, she's blushing! But, you see, why does this man frequent the collections? Is he inter-ested in the couture?"

"Well, I guess not really."

"Is he just going to see you?"

"Oh, no!"

"Mm-m. I must seem very curious to you, but that *is* one of my faults, I know. Still, it would be too bad if when you first come to Paris, you meet all the crazy people. If you do, you might never meet the normal people. I think that Hattie would tell you the same thing. For example, did you ever hear of Mr. Willi Hanke?"

Willi Hanke? What would anybody talk about, if it wasn't for Willi Hanke? He was beginning to seem like an old friend.

"That is simply the type I mean. A feminine. And he and his group were all wild, with a lot of money. Now, he liked to look at dresses because, perhaps . . . he wanted to wear them." She shrugged. "So, when I spoke to your friend, I wondered why does a young man like that go around to the collections? And you must forgive me, but I didn't want you to get involved. Absolutely. Not only am I Hattie's friend and I worry about you, but it could hurt you in Paris. Not that many people didn't like Willi Hanke. But he was . . . feminine."

"You mean, like a man-milliner?" I said in confusion.

She leaned forward to hand me a cigarette, and I saw from her face that she was perplexed now, too. She lit my cigarette and hers with a great big lighter set in some kind of plaster dwarf. She set it down and we heard steps. We both turned to see the old woman with two glasses on a tray coming slowly toward us down the narrow trail between divans and chests of drawers.

"Ah, thank you, Virginie. This is a sherry that Hattie brought us, Louise. This is how she and I have sat so many afternoons. And the first time, we had a few boys with us, didn't we, Virginie?"

Virginie nodded and smiled at me.

"They was both named Bill. *Were* both named Bill," said Florence. "Oh, that was funny. I was the only French, and my English was very bad. Does Hattie speak French anymore?"

"No."

"Of course. But she knew it very well, after so many visits over here. So many people fell in love with Hattie, because of her mistakes. She used to say *tu* to everyone—even Lucien Lelong! And when she'd go home, her friends in Paris still liked to repeat her mistakes. For example, you know the word *pauvre*? She used to say it like *pover*. When she saw the gypsies we have in Paris, she would say, 'Florence, I'm sorry to see all these povers everywhere. Where do they come from?' "

We all laughed, including Virginie, who was still with us.

Florence laughed again when she noticed this, and just as if we were alone, she said to me, "Virginie loves to remember Hattie. She keeps a picture of her in her room, don't you Virginie?"

At this, Virginie hurried away.

"She'll get the picture for you. She also has a Lazarus candy box, with the candies in it, still. From ten years ago! It's adorable. You can't imagine what Hattie means to her."

Florence leaned forward and said seriously, "Of all the friends I have brought into this house, only Hattie spoke to Virginie and shook her hand. Even those who come here often—they treat her like a wooden statue. They drop their coat in front of her, and they cry 'Florence, darling!' and they run in here to me! And why?" She sat back again and took up her sherry glass. "Hattie is a marvelous person. I *always* thought Hattie would marry, but she didn't. And she always thought *I* would marry, even though I told her no, I won't marry. So I would say, if you like marriage, why don't you do it? But she didn't want to, did she?"

"I don't know."

"Are you sleepy? Virginie can bring you some coffee, my dear."

I said I needed some, and she cried out to Virginie.

After this, we just sat a little while. I don't know if I was dozing, but I recall thinking, "Even way back here I can hear traffic." Then I heard a crash in the distance and I sat up. Florence was sitting there in a cloud of lamplight and cigarette smoke.

"It's just Virginie in the kitchen. She likes to get excited, instead of feeling useless. I do too sometimes! It doesn't matter who you are. But you'll see, when she brings the whole kitchen, and she will try to make the coffee so perfect. You'll see!"

I nodded in reply but was not very friendly because I was embarrassed at having fallen asleep in front of her.

"Get up! Please, feel free! You don't have to stick to that chair."

I stood up, thinking of Hedy, and of how little I resembled her, and I walked around the little patch of carpet by our chairs. There was a huge buffet at right angles to my chair, and I leaned on this and stared at a photo of a girl in a long ballerina skirt. She had her index finger up at her mouth as if to say "Be quiet." Below her feet it said,

> She was the Colonel's daughter
> Pet of the Aldershot Command.

Florence laughed in such a way that I knew it must be her, but as I felt cranky I didn't inquire.

"You seem very discontented," she said suddenly in a kind voice. "Is it because you didn't want to come tonight, or is it something bigger?"

"Oh, no, I wanted to come," I said weakly. "I'm just tired. Sorry."

"Why don't you tell me about the young man, then we can both stop worrying."

"He's just a guy I met. His name is Charles Gainsbourg."

"Charles de Gainsbourg? Oh, I see." She took my hand and patted it. "He goes for his father, am I right? His father makes fabrics? I know him, he's very nice. They are Jews, but very nice."

"That's what he told me." Then, defiantly, I said, "He doesn't care a bit about the clothes."

"Just stares all the time at you!" she said, putting her hands around her eyes like a pair of binoculars and laughing. I laughed, too, I wasn't sure at what, especially when she finished with "And I think you enjoy it, too. Yes, I think so."

A creaking sound became noticeable. I turned my head to see Virginie—away off in the distant part of the room where there were hardly any lights. She was pushing a tea wagon or something, with her head way down as if it was a load of ore being pushed around a mining camp. We sat and waited for her to arrive.

"It's fascinating," said Florence without lowering her voice in any way. "She is determined you will enjoy your coffee so much you will never forget us!"

Virginie was visible now. She passed by the other end of the buffet and made a right turn into the lamplight. She smiled but didn't stop until she had cried out, *"Attention, mademoiselle, les pieds!"* though she was nowhere near my feet.

Florence clapped her hands together and cried, "Bravo!" The tea table was covered with pitchers!

"Have you ever seen so many pitchers, Louise? This way, you can have your coffee perfect. Virginie is the only one who does the coffee this way."

159

"It looks awfully good."

After frowning and mixing things in a large American-size coffee cup, for which I was grateful, she stood aside to watch me drink. I nodded as much as I could, gave her the high sign, and finally we shook hands. She went away to close the curtains. Again it came to me, "I'm over here in Paris."

We went in to dinner after that, and I told Florence about the clothes I had seen. I began to have a lot of fun. I told her all my opinions, but she didn't advance any of her own. I told her about the suit with the buttons. She offered to have a copy of the shantung dress made for me, if I could let her see it. Making copies used to be her business, she told me, but the ready-mades had brought her to hard times even though, personally, she had "enough."

Virginie reappeared and Florence stopped. When she went away again, to the accompaniment of the creaking sound, Florence livened up suddenly and said, "And now—what do I hear? Lelong is making ready-mades himself! It's funny, really. He is lucky, too, because there is no more shortage of skilled seamstresses. They are pouring out of Germany and Poland and they need work so bad that he can have them for nothing. But Lelong is a nice man. I don't mean he is not a good man."

"You mean he makes them up and puts them on a rack in the middle of the showroom?"

"I don't know!" said Florence dramatically. "Mrs. Harrison Williams is going there, and Baba de Faucigny is going there! What do they say when they see each other there?"

"When they grab on to the same hanger, and get into a fight!"

"Ha. But Baba is short and the other is tall, so it might not happen. If only clothes could be made without fittings! That is why they go to the ready-mades. And now do you suppose the women who want to look like Mrs. Harrison Williams will bother to come out avenue Victor-Hugo to Florence, for three fittings and pay not bad money to her? No. Either they don't come, or they are already dead."

"Why don't you go on vacation and enjoy yourself, if you have enough yourself?"

"Yes, I have enough for myself, but some women who used to work for me, they don't have enough! Now, tell me about de Gainsbourg. How did you meet him? I hope he didn't bother you. The family is Jewish, of course."

I didn't see why she was harping on that, but I told her how he had sat by me at Chanel, and how the girl had come and taken his paper away, and how everyone there had stared at him.

She seemed very puzzled by it and asked me if Charles had been "making a little picture." I said yes.

"Is it possible he was just teasing the salesgirl and pretending to sketch? But nobody sketches anymore nowadays!"

"That's what it was. He was teasing them."

She was so excited she took a cigarette from my pack and we puffed away together. Finally she just laughed and said, "That is very funny. Those girls at Chanel annoy everyone. They are the *only ones* who don't know that Chanel herself hopes and wants to be copied. Every day and all the time."

Virginie came in and heard the story from beginning to end, and I was even able to follow by the hand gestures Florence made in her excitement. Virginie moved closer and closer, and presently was sitting down with us at the table. Not once did she move her eyes from Florence's smooth face. She laughed hard at the end and then spoke, in a ghost-story voice, asking Florence to ask me what exactly he had done when all the people turned around and stared at him. I said that he had turned and smiled at me. After we had the translation, we all laughed together, and Virginie pounded lightly on the table.

Now they knew for sure that he was no man-milliner man.

Then Florence explained that Virginie wanted her to tell me a story about an adventure she had had with Hattie one time. Virginie interrupted and Florence laughed.

"When Virginie was still as sexy as an actress, before she bent over." Florence blushed as she spoke.

Virginie nodded to me and I nodded back.

"Then I asked her who is bringing our dessert," Florence went on, "and she said the devil was bringing it."

Virginie looked so weak that I offered to get it.

"No, if you get it, she will blame herself for the rest of her life, and if I get it, she'll bicker with me. Look, she's pretending she doesn't see the plates."

Virginie interrupted by saying, *"Commencez, madame,"* in an angry voice. I knew enough to say *"Commencez,"* too, and bang my hand on the table. Then I added *"Tout de suite,"* which pleased them.

"Oh là!" Florence said. *"Je commence. Allez, Virginie, je commence.* One day, in 1925, in the early spring, I had to go to a lady in the Faubourg St.-Honoré. Virginie was to meet me later, because we had to go for fabrics and she had to help me carry what I bought.

"Now, Hattie was in town, and she was coming to see the fabrics with us. So, while I was with my client, Hattie and Virginie waited together at a table in a café. Where *normalement* Virginie did not like to go, but Hattie made her."

"Café Wepler," said Virginie.

"Café Wepler. *Alors,* soon a man came and he sat down with them and spoke to Hattie. He was an American man named . . ."

"Paul Johnson," said Virginie. Then she smiled charmingly and added, *"Des États-Unis."*

"Justement," continued Florence. "Paul Johnson said to

Hattie, 'Ain't you pretty?' but of course Hattie ignored him. But he didn't go away. Then a very handsome man walks by— a Frenchman with a beautiful suit. Hattie looked at him. Paul Johnson says, 'Now that's the type of foreigner I can't stand!' He said this, right in front of Virginie!"

I shook my head at Paul Johnson's mistake, and Virginie shook hers along with me. Florence sat back and took her reward, which was that Virginie was excited.

"Now, shall I get the dessert, Virginie?" she went on, pronouncing carefully and adding pantomime at the end.

"I go!" cried Virginie and left us.

I got up to get myself an ashtray, and then we ended up just wandering away from the table and back into the dim room with all the furniture. I could not imagine why there was so much or why Florence would tolerate it, since she was herself so well dressed and practical-looking. It was something like her devotion to Virginie, probably, who seemed like she would be a draining person to live with.

Florence invited me to look at the view, and so I kept going in pitch-darkness to the end of the room, and once there had to lift several kinds of curtains before I could get through to the glass. Below me I saw the stone yard, and beyond that, nothing but the beautiful arch, which was brightly lit and looked extremely close. I took the liberty of opening the window and was refreshed by the heavenly cool air.

When I was called back to the table, Florence asked me if I had been to Notre-Dame or the Sacré-Coeur. I said no, and that I never would this trip. I had a collection every day for three days, and the next day I went home. I told her I had to catch the *Berengaria* again.

"Maybe Hattie will let you stay longer, if you send her a wire. If you want to stay."

I stared at her and she stared back. Then she shrugged. "I think she would let you. Why not?"

"I don't know about Mr. Lazarus."

"Don't you think Hattie can arrange Mr. Lazarus?" she said, wobbling her head at me a little bit. "I don't see why not."

Though the idea of Hattie "handling" Mr. Lazarus offended me, the idea of staying was too fascinating to let go. I spent the rest of my visit standing by her little fancy desk while she wrote out crafty telegrams. As if Hattie responded to that kind of thing!

I have the final one here with me and it goes:

REQUEST ONE MORE WEEK PARIS STOP

WILL REIMBURSE STOP WILL LEARN A GREAT DEAL

It was my night for great monuments. I saw the Eiffel Tower in the cab going home—and for the first time it hit me. When I got into my room, I leaned out the window and saw it again. I was now too tired to go to sleep, and so I stayed there leaning and watching it, and hoping someone would take me to it. Didn't care who! I told myself.

I put on my nightgown, then sprawled some more on the windowsill, my feet on the little soft chair I had already spilled coffee on. I wasn't afraid. I realized that M. Danon saw something in me, and so did everybody in Paris. I hadn't known that thing as there, but it was, and I had better accustom myself to respect and lots of attention. That's what I told myself as I looked over the unknown city—a city I wouldn't have lasted in ten seconds, if I'd really been on my own.

I wanted to go to the Eiffel Tower because it was near the river, but just on the other side. I felt I needed several more hours down there. After all, France might go to war, or I might get married and get stuck in America. But would I ever marry a man who wouldn't let me go to Paris? He might kill me, and then he might be able to keep me from doing what I felt like!

I believed that a war caused by Germany was even less likely. Hitler had made an ultimatum, and then he'd thought it over and backed down. A real man-milliner. I'd barely heard of Mussolini, but I was pretty sure he was dying of syphilis. And, anyway, with Mussolini, all you had to do was present him with a plate of ravioli, wasn't that it? It would make him drop all his plans and sit down and eat. You could tell by looking at him that he was that kind. And then if he still wanted to fight, you could bring him meatballs. He was so simple he would even drop everything to hear a Chautauqua lecture such as: "What to Do Before the Doctor Comes."

At the top of the tower, there was one light only. The sky was light enough, though, that you could see the millions of dark bands. I felt romantic love for it, because it was so famous, yet it stood still for me to look it over carefully. There are several Arc de Triomphes around the world, but no one has built another one of these, unless you count the roof ornament on the City of Paris Department Store in San Francisco. Of the rest of the city, I could see just scattered lights and the glow from the Champs-Élysées. Not much later and it would be all dark, and all you could see would be cigarettes moving along.

Somewhere in the streets a man yelled *"Voilà."* It didn't sound like Charles, but, I told myself, it *could* be him. But that would mean he was out there with somebody else. So, it couldn't possibly be him.

Honey,

I've been thinking about you all day and I guess I'll start a letter. This is your third day on board. I just wish I could see you dancing up a storm with all the Continental men. I hope you've made some girlfriends.

I just bet you're dazzling all of them with your white coat.

I'll never forget the time you sat there at the kitchen table and told me you planned to have parties to go to every day, not just Saturday, and that maybe you could get your own place like Texas Guinan, except you didn't want that awful red hair. Course you've heard that story a million times. You were the smartest, cutest little girl I ever saw.

I got a letter from your mama this morning, which she sent off the day you left. They are just fine but she says they can't sleep for fear you'll be "submarined" by the Germans and also marry a foreigner. She says she's awfully sorry you ever took French.

The "Lux Hour" just went over. It's almost a miracle, isn't

166

it—having a whatyoucall 'em on the radio—who can throw his voice? I don't know as I think he's always all that funny all the time.

I'm sorry we didn't arrange for you to go over and see Mr. Marcel Rochas's collection, but it'll be the day before you arrive. Some of the buyers are interested, so I'd like to know what's with him. They say he only designs for the skinny girls. Perhaps there wouldn't be much demand for him out this way!

This morning Mr. Lazarus asked me how you were making out over in Paris. I told him you were doing just fine. It can't hurt! He's so afraid you won't understand the bank orders, but I know better.

By the way, dear, I mentioned to my friend Florence from the old days—I'm sure you've heard her mentioned—that you're coming out there, and I expect she'll call you. Don't worry about her! She's the nicest thing that ever walked.

Remember you kiss her on *both* cheeks.

I stopped and visited with your friend Betty today. She was telling me all about President Harding and his mistress, and the poor little baby they supposedly had.

I read the book but I never knew what to believe, did you? Of course it was way before your time. I can barely remember it myself. Your mama didn't believe a word of it, I seem to recall. It was the biggest thing that ever hit Ohio—that I do know—even though it's not saying very much.

Betty is missing you every day. She isn't happy in her home life, I guess. She's gotten into an argument with her father over a sign he hung up in the kitchen. It says, "What's Wrong with Our Apple Dumplings and Hard Sauce?" He wouldn't let her remove it. She wished she had a butter-and-egg man to come and take her out of it. I think she surprised both of us with that one.

She thinks Ellen Schutz wants to get rid of her and I'm afraid

167

that's true, but we know what Ellen's like. And I wouldn't be surprised if she was a little jealous of Betty's pretty face. Poor Ellen wouldn't tempt an anchovy, would she?

We are in the grip of a terrible hot spell. Oh, I forgot to say that we sent the blimp over with the new hours—just the regular fall hours—and it was so hot, somehow everybody thought it was going to puff up and float over east. Wouldn't that annoy them over in Wheeling! What if it floated over to Paris one day, and you looked up and saw it! Of course it would never get over the Maginot Line. *Ils ne passeront pas!*

Here's Red crying to go for his evening stroll, so I think I'll just conclude this tomorrow at the office. That'll mean a great saving in postage!

I think we might find Betty a different situation. I mentioned it to her and she cheered up quite a bit. She said she'd like that better than a pair of red blankets.

Just because I'm stopping writing doesn't mean I'm stopping thinking, darling.

XXX

Well, dear, here we are. I have a quarter of an hour, and I'll just do this, instead of thinking about the inventory.

Perhaps you didn't hear that Earl, our wonderful man in the stockroom, had to leave. It all seemed to happen in the middle of your going. His wife finally ran away, after ever so many close calls. I guess they were sitting there one evening, and she jumped up and said, "I must go to him," or something like that—just like in a play. But Earl doesn't know where the "him" is. Anyway, he had to go after her and swears he won't come back without her. They waited one week, but Earl's the head man, so they of course had to replace him. *Try*, anyway. Well, they got someone, and his name is Jenks! I wish to heaven you could see that man's eyebrows. They're as bushy and black as I don't know what. He reminds me of Bim Bam of Borneo, the dog-faced boy. I told him he didn't ever need to wear a hat to keep the rain out. He just beamed.

But he doesn't seem to want to do his work. When I ask him to do something for me, like I did last Saturday morning, for example, he just says, "I don't know about that. I've got an awful lot going on down here." I was so flummoxed I couldn't even speak, and you know that isn't like me. Have you ever heard of such a thing?

He says he used to work for the president of the Burlington and Ohio at his house in Burlington, which is a replica of a whole Pullman car. He told me so twice. I s'pose he feels he's ' come down in society.

I wanted to show his eyebrows to Mr. Lazarus, but Mr. Lazarus didn't want to meet him, so the other day when we had to send some things back downstairs I called for Mr. Jenks special, to bring the dolly up. Then I walked along with him toward the offices, by that way you can get to the freight elevator. I threw open the back door of Mr. L.'s office and I pushed him in. Mr. Lazarus was busy talking to some of the geegans from the accounting dept. Well, they all looked up and frowned good and hard at us with our dolly.

Then Mr. Jenks turned around and caught me pointing at his eyebrows. He was pleased as he could be! Then Mr. Lazarus, who didn't seem to be following it, asked us what we wanted. So I said, "Oh, Mr. Jenks just wanted to see the inside of your office." My, that was funny, but I hope Earl comes back soon.

It's mighty sad to think of that good man scouring all the bus stations up and down the country, solemn as a ghost. He says she kept a diary, and he was very funny about it. I'm not surprised either. I'll bet that diary would curl your hair. This is all between you and me, of course, and Earl and his wife. He says he couldn't find it. But if I know Earl, even if he found it, he'd take her back with never a word of reproach. Or will he just shake her a little and say, "You sweet idiot!" the way Fredric March did to his girl in that movie we saw! Remember?

I have some of the girls waiting to see me so I'll seal this up. My, but it's large. I'm glad *I* don't have to read it.

Oh, I forgot to tell you. There's a nice little boy here this morning. We can't find his mother. He's not the least bit down, not a bit of it! He says, Eddie Melton's my name and America's my nation! He's been sitting for three hours on Bessie Price's desk, reading "Happy Hooligan."

Well, I'll write again day after tomorrow. Before we even know it, you'll be home again. My, I wish I knew all your doings and how they're treating you! When you read this you'll have been all over Paris, and probably have learned the Apache dance!

Perhaps you could cable your mother, Louise. The man in the hotel—what's his name—he'll help you.

Hugs and kisses
Hattie

P.S. As Gert is on vacation I've been eating at the Good Humor. That poor red-haired boy whose heart you broke—you know the one!!—won't even look at me. Just looking at him makes me long to have you home, honey.

When I went back to Paris after the war, I realized how very easygoing that first trip of mine was. Other buyers were expected to get to three and four collections in a single day. Soon enough I was doing it myself—even crowding in the breakfast-time showings some furrier used to put on—I can't remember his name. I would sit there over a plate of hardening bacon, which didn't seem to be quite bacon, and exert myself to look at mountained-up furs on the stick-leg mannequins, who must have been feeling very hot. Fur salesmanship in those days usually tried to be humorous, mixing facts about the animals with what *you* could do in the coats. The sight of bacon on a plate still can bring this back to me.

Anyway, in 1938 I was oblivious of everything. I took my time in my fool's paradise, and it never dawned on me that those around me were in a race, and I was supposed to be in it, too. I suppose that's what annoyed Daphne Twomey.

So, the morning after my visit with Florence, when I saw it was raining, I simply decided to stay in till I had to go to Schiaparelli at two o'clock.

I dressed slowly in my copied Creed gray slacks, wondering how they might go over, and a white silk blouse. The maid hadn't ever come with my coffee, so when I dressed I went down to demand some.

The dining room—where I had never been before—was a small, dark place at this hour, with a frieze of nude girls running around at eye level—painted on to look like Wedgwood. They ran in single file, each one reaching for what the girl in front of her had. But they all had the same thing, anyway—it was a bunch of ribbons.

There was a dressy old couple eating, and otherwise the room was empty. I expected to hear the kitchen was closed. But there was nothing like that. A very young girl brought me coffee and a brioche without a word, then left me alone. Though it was nearly noon, the lobby and dining room were hushed and cozy.

I wondered if I would see the famous Schiaparelli in person today, and if she'd come up and try to scare me with her skunk-fur coat. It's a marvel how I continued to think all these big-name couturiers were sitting around with nothing but me on their minds.

But Charles had singled me out. I went over all my memories of him—how the backs of his hands looked, the way he leaned back on his Humber, how long his legs were, and the part of his neck and chest that I could see when his collar wasn't buttoned. Desire was new to me. So I said to myself, "Charles has such beautiful clothes."

I saw M. Danon pass by in the lobby. He happened to see me, too, and he waved a newspaper he was carrying and came in. The other people smiled at him and he veered a little their way, and they all said things that sounded like bird chirps, the old lady in particular.

When he got to my table he smiled and said, "They are Italian people," and handed me the paper.

"Shall I send the waitress to you?" he continued, folding his hands and bending his body toward me like a puppet. When I declined, he made a little humorous bow and left the dining room. He was wide across the back—maybe four or five times wider across the back than Charles. What did his wife think about it? It was a strange thing in a man! Of course he was ever so much older. But I really couldn't imagine that a hundred years would ever make Charles wide like that.

I looked over the front page of the Paris *Herald*, which was the paper M. Danon had thoughtfully brought me, avoiding words like "Sudetenland" and "Chamberlain"—anything that had to do with politics. Much more important, it seemed to me, was the news of Howard Hughes's round-the-world flight and whether it had possibly been a hoax! Then I saw the little item on General Hugh Johnson. That was "Ironpants" Johnson, the guy my father wanted to shoot! Ironpants Johnson of the New Deal and the NRA. I could picture him rolling down dirt roads in a jeep; he'd be forced to stand all the way because of his pants, but he'd keep his balance by gripping the windshield and thrusting out his chin!

Then, back home it would be, "Dinner, Ironpants! Salmon loaf and creamed peas!" Or, "Oh, Ironpants, make love to me!" Or she might tell her girlfriends, "I *never* wear low-cut dresses. My Ironpants gets too jealous."

M. Danon came back in from the lobby. This time he seemed to be in no hurry. He nodded again at the old people, who were sitting at their table like statues.

"*Alors, mademoiselle,*" he said, coming to stand across the table from me, "I hope your business trip is going very well."

My primitive manners told me to nod at least, and I did, but I wondered if he was about to launch into something about either Charles, or Charles being a Jew, or Willi Hanke. I just felt he was on the verge of one of those subjects. So I said, "I see Ironpants Johnson is here in the paper! Front page!"

"Is it so!" he said. He unfolded his hands and came around to look. "General Johnson will be staying here in our hotel. Does it say so in the paper? Let me see. No, I don't think so. A pity!"

" 'General Hugh Johnson, known as Ironpants'—I love this *Herald*, really!" he said with a laugh, glancing at me. "Never too solemn. 'General Hugh Johnson, known as Ironpants, the current chief of the National Recovery Administration, has been asked by President Roosevelt to stop in Paris. . . .' Oh, but they don't mention the Élysée Palace." He put the paper down by my plate after carefully folding it. "No doubt it is a question of security. *Eh bien, mademoiselle!* I hope Paris pleases you. I only am sorry it has to rain while you are here."

"I did mean to go down to the river today. Down by the Eiffel Tower."

"Ah, of course we will find you an umbrella, and of course a taxi, but perhaps this afternoon would be better. The rain may stop."

"Hm," I said, not looking at him. I thought he was disagreeable.

173

"And have you seen the tower at night from your window? You can see it quite easily. It is the room Monsieur Lazarus always has, for that reason. He is very fond of it. Please tell me, by the way, how is my dear friend?"

"Oh, he's well," I said. Mr. Lazarus and I weren't on the close footing M. Danon seemed to think. I wouldn't know if he was well or not, unless Hattie happened to say he had a cold. In fact I'd be embarrassed to think he wasn't well, because Mr. Lazarus was like a god around the store. M. Danon went on smiling as if he expected something, so I told him about the car that had crashed into one of the big windows at the front of the store, and how Mr. Lazarus had them put a sign above it saying, "Everything Comes to Lazarus." "And once a year he gives a tea party for everyone over eighty," I concluded.

"*Ah! Une belle idée! Magnifique,*" said M. Danon. "I admire his brilliant thinking always. There is really no other way to describe it, *mademoiselle.*" He threw his head back and looked up at the ceiling, as if trying to put the whole thing into words.

"You see, I am sure that every customer at his store *knows* that Monsieur Lazarus cares for him. This is good business— much harder to achieve in a large department store than in a small hotel, by the way, and yet . . . And he is a very kind friend, Monsieur Lazarus, as well!—I'm sure you know, *mademoiselle,* as well as I do. When we received his request for a room for you, *mademoiselle,* Monsieur Lazarus's assistant had written in *great* detail, on two long pages, all that should be done to make you comfortable in Paris, including your schedule of visits, and that you must have coffee in your room"— here he paused as if at the grandeur of the idea—"so that you would not go back to sleep!"

He was still standing by my chair, but it was as if his mind had gone up into some incredible place in the clouds.

"And then, underneath, in his own handwriting, Monsieur Lazarus wrote, 'Take care of Miss Merrill, won't you, Danon? Best, Lazarus.' It's the Monsieur Lazarus way, *mademoiselle*," he went on, smiling warmly at me. "Most attractive for business."

"Well," I said, "we all like him in Columbus. We think a lot of him."

"Well, I must go and look into the kitchen. Soon, the people who come expecting lunch! Excuse me, and do not hurry."

I watched him receding again, only this time it was through a pair of swinging doors into the kitchen. Probably his wife never even thought about his hips—didn't have time because the man talked so much. I got up to go and check the weather out in the street, and of course I thought about Hattie and the attractive way *she* had.

I went over the turquoise rugs to the wide brass doors that always stood open, and where a kind of doorman stood, just out of the reach of the rain. It was terribly invigorating there. Even though the rain hurt my plans, I wanted to be near it. The cabs and cars almost splashed us, and you could barely see the other side—only the striped awnings straight across were visible. And the noise seemed unnatural and violent. You couldn't believe the drops weren't killing someone.

In fact, while I stood there, hugging my arms, and even forgetting I had slacks on, I was being hooted at by the man behind the desk, but not hearing him. It took the doorman, or taximan is what he actually was, tugging on my sleeve to rouse me and turn me toward the desk.

"There is a message for you, Mademoiselle Merrill."

I went over sort of coolly, and took the note without thanking him. I'd suddenly remembered I had slacks on, and thought he might have been staring at me while I was looking out the door.

It was a folded-up note from Charles.

> May I come for you tomorrow at noon? We'll go to Balmain together if you have to go, but first an hour by the river. I hope you will. Unfortunately today I have to work (a meeting, and my father is away from Paris).
>
> Love, Charles

I put this away. I had never gotten anything so beautiful, especially if you read the ending first. "What a Mensch," I told myself. "What a Mensch." I didn't know what it meant— I just knew it was Jewish and it was good, and it helped me to keep from blaming him.

I went back to stand by my anonymous friend the taximan, who was peering and squinting at the rain with a tiny cigarette butt between his lips. I felt he didn't want to appear anxious to get me a cab, if I didn't really want one, so he didn't look at me, and I didn't look at him.

Now, though I knew Charles wasn't coming, I kept leaning way out to see if I couldn't catch sight of him. I did see a group of rich-looking men in suits come along the sidewalk toward us, all hunched down under their black umbrellas. There was a large one in the lead, and he held his umbrella ahead of him as if it were a flag. The others followed, as if they were just there to carry his briefcase. I thought this might be Ironpants, out of uniform for security reasons—come to check in with his brain trusters. Did the taximan know? He'd been forced to lean way out, too, because of me, and now his head was wet.

He was called out to the street by a scream. A taxi had pulled up to the door and splashed the man I thought was Ironpants. All one side of him was wet, and he stood striking at the water on his coat. Then he looked up—perhaps to curse the ones in the taxi. They were a dressed-up couple of women who were just at that moment running past him, giggling and unconscious of it all. I looked back at Ironpants, expecting an explosion of rage! I was surprised to see that Ironpants was a bizarre, short-haired woman. She straightened up and made some kind of disgusted comment in a foreign language, and they all walked on in their pants and tie shoes.

"*Hermaphrodites,*" said the taximan.

I had to get ready, so I went back to my room and dressed in my white linen dress again—leaving on my flat shoes. I also decided to wear no coat and to tie up my hair any which way. I was dressing for the river—for the river lying flat in the sunshine. But I wasn't too foolish to borrow the umbrella on my way out.

I knew that dressing this way was bound to get me stared at among the buyers, for whom clothes and makeup were like mummy wrappings, or coats of paint. It would seem insane to them, or some might think I was looking for a new way to get noticed. I just prayed the weather would clear.

At the last minute I put my invitation in my purse and was dismayed to see in there the telegram I'd forgotten to send, on the thick pink paper that had come out of the cubbyhole in Florence's little desk. "It's not enough to write these things," I told myself. "You also have to send them." Or say good-bye to Charles day after tomorrow.

I ran all the way downstairs, and then hurled myself on the man at the desk. He gave me a pen, and I wrote out Hattie's address. Then he took the paper and read out each word—

loud enough for everyone in the lobby to be able to consider the pros and cons of my staying. He assured me it would go directly. I stared into his eyes. Then I forced myself to go on out the door, where the taximan was waiting in the rain to get me a cab and hand me an umbrella—an umbrella that had once belonged to a person named Edward Forbes. Then I was whisked away to Schiaparelli in the place Vendôme.

THERE WERE mostly "up" hairdos in the collections that year. Most designers—not Chanel, of course—had built their collections around that look. What I recall most vividly about this show was the choice Schiaparelli had made in this. She wasn't content to brush the back straight up and show the unappealing nape of the neck, which was the main innovation of the style. She pulled it straight back off the forehead, too (except for one mannequin with jet-black hair who had it fixed in two sinister bumps above her temples). The effect was startling to everybody, even though many in the audience themselves had up hairdos by this time. It's these hairdos that stick in my mind now. They were too new. They were like what you saw on immigrant women in newsreels about Ellis Island, when the women sat crying in despair at the results of their tuberculosis tests and their head scarves slipped off.

But the clothes were astonishing, too. Jackets weren't fitted and shoulders were wide. The models' heads looked like tiny, mean BBs! (What would Charles have said? I was already wondering.) There were huge ceramic buttons on all blouses and suits and—this being Schiaparelli—on evening dresses, too. Fabrics were printed with paintings of things like gears and shovels. By the end I felt I had aged one hundred years. I didn't buy but went away discussing the whole thing with Hattie and Charles in my mind. We all agreed that Schiaparelli was making fools out of women, and on purpose.

Unfortunately for me it was still raining hard when I came out of the show. I went a few paces with my large umbrella, but I couldn't kid myself for long. Besides, the thought that Daphne Twomey might be in one of the taxis that were whooshing by me and sending up a dirty spray decided me to get a cab of my own and go back to my hotel. And I thought Charles might try to get me on the phone. I opened the shutters when I got inside, and with the banging of the rain to entertain me, I undressed and lay down to think about him and what his life might be like.

Being Jewish, he and his family might wear those small caps while in the house, even if they didn't seem to wear them on the outside. They'd have strange cookies, monotonous singing, and those things no one ever talked about which went along with Jews. I saw myself eating dinner with them and being aware of these things hanging in the air above the table. His father, in a long beard, would seem to be glaring at me. But Charles would explain that he *had* to do it, to all newcomers.

It was quite breezy in the room, and I got under the covers. I saw the sky begin to get dark. The rain kept falling. In the midst of the noise, I heard pigeons cooing, where they were hiding themselves under the little balcony that wasn't even large enough to put your feet on. *"Il y a du monde au balcon,"*

I thought. It doesn't really mean "There are folks on the balcony." It means "She has big breasts." Hattie had told it to me.

The phone woke me up at six-thirty. It was the man at the desk, calling to say that I had two visitors. "They are asking to see you," he went on harshly, as if he thought they were asking too much.

Then I heard, away off in the distance, "It's Dan, honey! Old Harry, too!"

"I'll be there!" I screamed and hung up on the deskman. *This* should be fun. I jumped up and started to tear around the room, pulling things off their hangers. "*Will* it be fun, though?" I wondered as I went. Had Dora come to see me too? I wasn't discussing Jean with her, if that was what she wanted!

I slammed down my Pigeon's Blood lipstick on the tile beside the sink. Here I was in my slip, my hair all brushed, my wrinkled dress all picked out. Was it so I could sit miserably on a wooden chair, with Harry on one side and Dora on the other, and both of them pouting? I belonged to Charles now! Terribly mixed up for a moment there, I started to cry, thinking of Charles in one of those dear little caps. I pulled myself together, but as a matter of principle I didn't fuss too much with my makeup. Dan might help keep Harry off, but he'd pretend not to see what Dora was up to. I'd thank him for stopping Harry and I'd say, "But, Dan, somehow I still don't feel just right."

And there'd be Dora pawing at me! Or would I just shove her—hard enough that she fell over backward in her chair? I thought how handily Ed would manage everything, if only he were here. Nothing escaped him, and he was never afraid. I trusted him just as I trusted Hattie and Charles. But unlike Hattie and Charles, I'd probably never see him again.

I cried then, and all during my ride in the elevator, as I thought about Ed and Jean. They should know how happy I was. But of course that was silly because they'd probably forgotten who I was. I don't know how tear-stained I looked when the doors opened, but I couldn't figure out a way to keep them closed. Anyway, my first sight was Dan—no one at his side—telling a story with gestures to the deskman, but the deskman wasn't looking up.

"An', an' I knew the guy wasn't a real Parisian," he was saying. "Louise! Mary! Honey!"

I hurried over and got bear-hugged. He told me I was a sight for sore eyes, and I told him he was. I really was happy to see his same square face again with the wrinkles around the eyes. He looked just like a policeman in a comedy, who smiles at the end when the lovers get together.

He took my hand and we started toward the doors. "Come on over here—I want to show you somebody." He tugged twice on my arm. "Hey, how you *been?*"

Just then the deskman ran around in front of us and handed me a telegram and a little pen to sign with.

"Say, what can it be?" Dan murmured. "Not war, I hope!"

The message wasn't signed, but it had to be from my father.

HOT HERE STOP DONT LIKE TO THINK OF
YOU FLYING IN PLANES

"Everything okay at home?"

I nodded, and he said to come on—that it was somebody right over here who was waiting just for me!

"Is it Dora?"

"Why no, honey. Dora couldn't come tonight, I'm afraid. But look here."

He pointed his finger out the street door. "It's this fella."

182

Harry, who was leaning on a brass fireplug and smoking a cigarette, turned around and showed us his sulky expression.

"He's a little shy, though, honey," said Dan sincerely. And to Harry he went on, "Well, son, don't you know who you're looking at?"

"Hello, Louise," he said, standing up.

"Let's get out of here and get some supper! You know, I've had some good food in Paris so far."

We hit the sidewalk and walked in a hurry, with Dan in the middle. "We thought we'd just eat at some little place, y'know, then go take in this little club I know—the Aurore. Ever heard of it? You can't beat it, that's all. We'll have a good time. My, I'm glad you were in. You look bright as a button. Heard anything of our ship friends? We had a real big time, didn't we, on that old boat?"

"It's so good to see you, Dan," I said, giving him a jab around the ribs. "I can't believe it's only been a week."

"I know it. And I've spent most of that time going through some hellish museums. Seen more than I can stand, actually. What's Harry doing back there?"

We turned back around. Harry was well behind us, walking as slowly as possible and looking about him as if the whole place was dirty. Seeing us, he slowly caught up and finally joined us, stopping the other side of Dan. I knew what he wanted, but I didn't have it in me.

"Heard any bad news from home?" he said, leaning forward around Dan to see my face.

"No," I replied. "Why should I?"

"Financial news, I mean," he said.

Dan chuckled. "I'll be damned if that doesn't sound like the start of a real good joke I knew once. 'Heard the financial news?' " He laughed, but we couldn't really join in, and then he started to whistle. Two women in aprons who were taking the air at the door of a shop looked him up and down. The streetlights popped on, and we got walking again. I really hoped a restaurant would come along soon so that I could have some coffee.

Occasionally, when a car went by, Dan and I would lurch to the left to avoid getting sprayed from the gutter. It was an inconvenience to Harry, who was on the inside. After a time or two I started to feel bad, so I said, "What financial news were you talking about before, Harry?"

"Oh," he said, "it's Federated Department Stores. Their bond rating has slipped pretty fast the last few months. Everybody seems pretty pessimistic."

"Boy, maybe I better quit." I glanced at Dan, expecting him to laugh. But he was frowning.

"You know, Harry, there *was* that old joke about Hoover and Mrs. Hoover, and he asks her about the financial news. . . . Then it's . . . something, something, and she says—what was that, dang it all? 'Sunshine men stay out!' That was the punch line. Mrs. H. to Mr. H.: 'Sunshine men stay out.' " He laughed.

"Before my time," said Harry.

"I bet it was a damn good joke if you had all of it," I said.

Dan nodded and said it was a honey, and then Harry—who had reached the cross street—turned around and demanded to know what we were doing. "Seems damn stupid, just walking around like bums."

We went across, and it so happened there was a little place on the next corner—dark inside, but with a man in an apron watching us from way in the back. We peered in, expecting him to beckon or wave as you might expect a restaurant owner to do. But he just stared back at us.

"Come on, I know it's open," said Dan in a commanding voice. "We'll get a couple of them *steak frites* nice and quick, and then we'll go on up and hit that place I was telling you about, the Aurore."

I sat between them on a wooden banquette, and we ate without too much talking. I think we were tired from our reunion. The restaurant wasn't interesting—not fancy or luxurious, like a tourist place, and not happy and loud like a *brasserie* either. The staff all looked like members of one family, and all gave off disappointment. I don't know whether with us or with the restaurant business. Probably they weren't making much profit in that expensive district but were still hanging on out of spite.

When Dan laid down his fork and asked me did I "want a *gâteau* or something," I not only said no but I jumped up off my seat, where I was forced to stand in a bent posture till the other two got up.

"She's chomping at the bit! Wants to get out there and break some hearts," Harry said as we filed out of the booth.

"I'll get this, Harry, boy," said Dan. "And as for Mary— you just keep your mind on little Miss Whatsername and you won't get hurt." He laid some bills in the palm of the waiter's hand, then did the tip separately, saying, "There, there, and there, my man." He put his wallet inside his jacket and chuckled to me, "This money feels like a wad of circus posters."

He laid his hand on my back and we started toward the door. "Now I'll show you two something lively."

Out on the street he waved us a cab, and when it obeyed, that party feeling began to creep up on me. So much so that, leaning back into the soft seat, with Dan's hand over mine and Harry sulking opposite us in the little seat, I went a little nutty and said, "So what's Dora doing tonight?"

"Oh, Dora's at the hotel, havin' in some friends she met at a store. She's havin' a real big time over here, I'm glad to say."

"She thinks Dan's at a Masons' meeting tonight," said Harry, without taking his eyes away from the flying street scene.

"Well, I guess that's true," said Dan quietly. "But, hell, I can see Masons any day of the week back home." And after a second he added in my ear, "And Masons aren't exactly my idea of Paris."

"Lucky for him the meetings are secret," said Harry. "It's a good alibi for a married man."

Dan laughed. "And I'm spared a bunch of Washington ladies from the Progress Club, and I get to see my little friend Mary, who's cute as she can be. Now if only Ed and his gal were along."

A snort came from over by Harry.

"I miss them—boy, do I," I said, sighing.

"That boy couldn't keep his mouth shut to save his life!" exclaimed Dan. "Was he really a Socialist, do you suppose, or was he really just a dyed-in-the-wool Republican like you and me? My God, he used to make me laugh!"

He laughed and I got laughing, too, and in the midst of it, Dan cried, "But did you see that fella play piano? Why it could have been one of those European dudes! I couldn't *believe* it was our joker friend who'd been leaping around all day."

"He's nothing but a rah-rah boy," said Harry. "You see them crawling all over Yale. Publicity hounds!"

"Sure, Ed wants to be the Screen Gems Glamour Man of the Year," I said, "so he actually pretended he could play the piano."

Harry turned to me, mad. "You know what I mean. He's also a sex fiend—but maybe some people like that."

I said, "Hah!" or something. The party atmosphere was dissipating, but Dan saved it by not hearing us. Instead of joining in, he shouted, "That's the ticket!" and slapped my

186

knee. We'd pulled up to an unusual neon-lit doorway, with a small sign that said "L'Aurore."

Harry jumped out and paid, and Dan and I lumbered out any old way—perhaps just giddy that Harry was a little way off.

L'Aurore was a pretty place—the sign was pretty, anyway— the lights representing the dawn. The stone building was surprisingly dignified, with little bushes beside the door. A man in livery was holding the door for some laughing, well-dressed couples. As we came up behind them, Dan murmured, "The white tie and tails gang, Mary. There's plenty of 'em here. It's a wonderful little spot. Heard about it from back home. Spent most of last night here, too!"

I nodded to him and peeked in as the doorman swung the heavy door. I saw soft lights and heard accordion music. That surprised me a little bit. If only Harry would leave us alone, though, it could be fun.

"Harry thinks the world owes him a living," I said to Dan.

"Well, I know he does," Dan replied, "but he'll outgrow it."

He came up behind us right then, as the maître d' jumped down from his little podium and came over.

"*Messieurs, 'dames,*" he said softly. We followed him through the hundred onlookers at their candlelit tables all littered with drinks. In front of us on the stage, a band was playing—an unusual band of overweight men in splashy uniforms. One had a tuba, but I think all the rest were accordions. The music sounded wholesome, sort of a strange kind of thing for Dan to want, I thought, on nights he'd sneaked away from Dora.

All in all, it was quite refined for a nightclub. The walls had silk panels in sea-foam green, with flower garlands in the center, and the room was lit with nice little chandeliers.

Dan winked as we sat down and ordered three whiskey and sodas. "Clever heads call for Calvert whiskeys," he said with a chuckle when the waiter had gone.

"Well, I'm not sure I wanted any," said Harry.

"Why, be my guest," said Dan, waving his arms. "You do the ordering, *I'll* do the paying."

"The man's a saint!" I cried.

"In that case I'll have champagne," said Harry.

"Good idea," said Dan. "Wish I'd thought of it."

Now we all lit up one of Harry's Woodbine cigarettes. Dan and I asked him, "Where'd you get these?" at exactly the same second, and Dan had to say some rhyme to bring good luck. "This is the life," said Dan, leaning back. "This is Paris, everything deluxe. That band," he explained, pointing, "is Monsieur Gladerewsky and His All-Cossack Band. A pretty famous outfit in this part of the world."

"I thought you liked jazz, though, Dan."

"Oh—all kinds! I like all kinds. And there's the cook—we get him to come out later. He's an American and he plays superb. Last night he came out around two A.M., and he played 'Only Make Believe.' It reminded me of that soiree we had on the ship."

Our drinks arrived and Harry arrived right behind them. He'd been wandering around somewhere. He tended right to his drink now, and I watched him, fascinated as before by his trembling hands. I remembered how he'd said he felt like a thing in evening clothes for me to spit on. I guess he felt that way now, too, but I wasn't going to think about it.

"So what's that hotel of yours like?" he said, looking up. "What was the name?"

"The Royal Palace!" cried Dan.

"The Élysée Palace," I said. "It's where Ironpants Johnson stays."

"What's he doing in Paris?" said Dan.

"Probably just a stopover on his way to Russia. Wants to find out how he can get more graft into the New Deal."

They laughed pretty hard.

"Where are you two staying?"

"I'm at the Splendid," said Harry. "But I may change. Dan's at the Florida. Says the rooms are bigger."

"Come on, Mary. What say we dance?" said Dan. "Let Harry sit and think about his responsibilities."

"What?" I said. Harry was blushing.

"He's engaged, Mary. Been engaged all this time, and never told a soul."

"Well, it's not your particular business, that I know of."

I congratulated him and he lit up another cigarette.

"Don't worry," called Dan as we moved toward the dance floor. "I'll fill her in while we're dancing."

"How are we going to dance to this tuba music, Dan?"

"Oh, we'll just waltz around. You'll see."

When we got to an empty part, he took hold of me and held me close. His red face had no expression. Along with all the other couples, we were soon swirling around to the corny rhythm. "It's a nice place, Dan."

"I knew you'd like it, honey. I thought of it when I was here last night, and they played 'Only Make Believe.' "

He started singing "Only Make Believe" and I joined in. We weren't troubled by the tuba music. I was thinking of our time on the ship, and just as Charles had blotted all that out, and the ship had blotted out home, now this almost blotted out Charles.

I thought of Jean and Ed, and started pining for them. I also pined for Wentworth, and I missed the scornful feeling Mrs. Dicky had aroused in me.

If there was no change of plan, I'd be back on that wonderful ship in forty-eight hours, and steaming toward the *Ambrose*. Possibly with Wentworth's paternal hand on my shoulder. I would have thought differently, but I was a damned fool.

The music stopped some time before Dan and I gave up swaying together. I know it because eventually a young woman came up behind me and stood there facing Dan. I couldn't see her, but I heard her *"Bonsoir,"* and I realized the music had stopped.

I heard his reply, too, which was "Well, *bonsoir*, Eva!"

He introduced her, pronouncing her *"ma petite amie*, Eva." The two of us shook hands, and I told her my name was Louise—getting it in before Dan could say it was Mary. She looked at me with big brown eyes that had a startled expression.

We walked back to the table while they had some kind of conversation. Dan sounded jolly, but she sounded very intense.

Eva was heavy, and her silver halter dress didn't flatter her very much. Harry scowled at her while being introduced, but neither Dan nor Eva seemed to notice.

"I saw Eva here last night," said Dan when we'd all sat down. "She's just a little girl, she was all on her own and standin' over there. We danced all night, till the waiters had to change their clothes, and that wasn't till round about four A.M.! Lucky for us she's got connections!" He turned around to smile in her face, and take her hands in both of his.

She appeared to blush a little, and tucked her chin way down into her neck.

"My father is . . . that waiter," she said, pointing off somewhere into the distance.

Harry groaned loudly. "Care to dance, Louise?"

I agreed, and we left the strange couple behind us. Out on the floor Harry took me in his arms quite tightly. I might have minded, but by now I knew the routine. And the routine was especially funny if he really was engaged.

L'Aurore seemed to have its special clientele, made up of heavy people with fair hair. One of them made a little scene near us. She and her partner kept right after another couple like themselves. I imagine they were her husband and her best girlfriend. Laughing like mad, she'd grab at the fabric covering the man's behind, and then they'd all scream till the little flower tiara fell off her head and had to be rescued from among everybody's feet.

"Thinks she's Shirley Temple," said Harry. "But she weighs in at—let's see—five hundred and fifty pounds. Trust Dan to find a place like this. And drag us along. 'Course I don't think the band is what lured him back."

"Are you really engaged, Harry?"

"No comment."

"I'll still let you dance with me. I understand. This must be one of those trips you get sent out on before you're married, so you can live it up before you . . . go back and put on the yoke. In Lake Placid."

"Lake Placid! I'm from Lake Forest."

"Oh, what a terrible mistake."

That song ended. I untangled Harry's arm and stepped away from him. Nobody was leaving the dance floor, but I was willing to go back.

"Let's stay here." Harry jerked my hand back. "Dan and the little princess don't want us."

I peered over there, and in fact Dan was curled right around Eva, and they looked as if it was the most engrossing night of their lives.

"We don't want to go over there and frighten the little girl," Harry continued wittily. "She's *only* thirty-five years old. She only has five or six kids."

The accordions plunged into "Cielito Lindo," and we re-sumed our fox trot.

"So—you could never really stand me, could you?" Harry said.

"Are you trying to annoy me?"

He snorted.

"Let's just talk about something else."

"Like what?" he said in a mean voice.

I looked up into his pale face, which was now all red. The laughing people bounced all around us. So many of the women had floating panels to their dresses, I noticed.

"Well," I said, "do *you* know what to do before the doctor comes? Or, I wonder what Ironpants Johnson could be doing in Paris? Want to talk about it?"

"Probably on his way to assassinate somebody for his President."

"You've got a screw loose."

"Well, they did in Huey Long. Why stop there? The American people are too dumb to notice."

"Oh, let's just go back."

"Dan will tell you the same thing," said Harry, following behind and almost laughing at the obviousness of it. "The guy was overheard!"

"This band's about to go over," said Dan excitedly as he got up to pull out my chair. "Then they call the cook. He's what they call full of hop, Mary. They bring on a special piano—all the lights go down, and he plays 'Mad About the Boy'—or whatever you ask him to! He's a Negro fella. Not but what this type of music is good in its own way, too."

"Could you give me a cigarette, Dan?"

"Sure, honey, here. Say, what's Harry done to Eva?"

Eva was coming toward us, having been out to powder her nose. She must have encountered Harry on her way back, because though near her, he was going off in the other direction, and she looked mad. She'd put on a net shawl that stood up around her shoulders. I was startled to see that *her* dress had floating panels, too, attached at the waist with rosettes. Actually, I saw as she came closer, the dress was brocade.

"Dan! What he said to me!"

"What, what'd he say to you, pumpkin?" Dan stood up.

She put her hands over her face. "Can't tell you in front of Louise."

"Dan, I have to go back," I said, getting up. "I had a great time."

"We'll take you in a cab, honey. I won't hear of it."

"We'll take you in a cab," said Eva. "It's no trouble."

"You don't want to miss the cook, though, do you?" I said, getting my coat on. "And perhaps Eva's father wouldn't want her to leave."

They stood there with Dan's arm holding them together in one package—Dan's excited face red and square, and Eva's far below it, sort of a dark crimson color.

"I'll be fine, you two," I said gaily. I blew a kiss to Dan and hurried toward the curtained door that led out to the entrance. The All-Cossack Band was playing "Loch Lomond," but why, or how they ever danced to it, I don't know.

The deskman was looking out for me when I got back. He handed me a folded letter. It was on blue paper. Charles. The man saw my face and turned the other way to be discreet. I didn't even care but ran and sat down to read it.

My dearest Louise,

Is it possible to miss someone so much I only met three days ago? This afternoon Lelong was humming that foolish

song, "When two kisses blend in one . . ." You know it?
I stopped our meeting just to make him tell me all the words.
Now I can sing it all day with you in my mind.

I hope it went well with you. I regret very much missing our
day. I hope you did not get wet in the rainstorm we had, and
that you found the clothes terribly exciting. I hope that Miss
Tunney didn't find you, and finally I hope that no one else
found you either, because I want you to belong to me.

Though I don't expect you to feel the way I do, I can tell
you my feelings—since you are so kind. As well as beautiful
and brave . . .

À *demain*
Charles

I read this letter many times and marveled that it should
have been addressed to me. Then in ecstasy I folded it and
stood up to go to my room. And at that moment Harry was
coming through the door, smiling and kind of hugging a woman,
and walking her across the lobby to me. He was calling my
name, looking as radiant as a bride.

"We're here to say we're sorry!" he exclaimed. "We didn't
mean it all those times. We're just so damn . . ."

He put out his hand to me and pulled me to him. "It's
crazy, isn't it, how people like me get?" he said. All three of
us shook our heads and laughed, his girlfriend going along
with it happily. Her nose was something like a pig's nose,
where you can look straight into the nostrils. She was sweet,
though. She was just as drunk as Harry was.

"Look, I don't . . ." he began, and shook his head sincerely,
"I don't . . ."

"It's okay, Harry, whatever it is!"

"I don't," he began again with a bewildered look.

When he didn't finish, I laughed again, and he and the girl laughed. Then, most unlike him of all, he suddenly took his leave.

"We've really got to go," he said, raising his hand benignly. "You know how to get to your hotel and everything, don't you?"

"Oh, we're fine! Fine isn't the word for it!"

They turned as one person. Harry's arm was keeping his friend's head at an angle, and I'm sure she couldn't move it, but she smiled all the same. As they neared the door, Harry's gestures showed he was already making plans how to open it.

I called out " 'Bye" once more, feeling gay and happy. I went upstairs with my letter—no thoughts to spare for the man and his transformation.

Dear Louise,

When you read this you'll be all ready to come home, and I can't wait.

I just want to tell you to remember for sure to pay your hotel with one of your American Express money orders because your Lazarus bank orders are for COUTURE only.

I must hustle, but I want to tell you that as I dropped Mr. L. at the train this morning and I was looking out the window along Division Street, I saw a family hoeing cabbages between the river and the tracks, and it just made me think of your poor mother and father. Well, I'm making a hash of this but you know what I mean.

Do be sure to remember to bring them home something *nice*. I know you would anyway, darling.

You can use your American Express and we'll work it out later.

Just received your sweet letter from on-board. Miss you.

Hugs and kisses

Bon voyage!

Hattie

Don't forget to let us know by wire when you'll arrive.

I found this letter on my dresser next morning. All that about American Express seemed to have sealed my fate, but I told myself it didn't mean much, really. I went down for some coffee. The maid had probably seen all she wanted to see and didn't care to come up anymore.

Of course I was preoccupied with whether there would be a reply to my wire. If they were going to tell me I couldn't stay, I hoped the reply wouldn't be there yet, to ruin our last day. I mean that I hoped the way you hope the rain clears off so you can go swimming.

I didn't really count my father's message as a reply—it seemed more like a random warning. Probably he'd heard about a plane crash—maybe the one his cousin had, and soon he was picturing me climbing into a plane and waving from the plane's window with a doomed look on my face. Within a few days his anxiety would get so great he'd just have to get it off his chest and send me a telegram, after which he'd forget all about it. He'd even forget that people *rode* on planes; he'd tell you to your face that planes were for freight.

I stepped into the elevator after two fashionable American women. None of us had any room in there, but that didn't keep them from their tense conversation, which was carried on with many pauses. They weren't even self-conscious.

The doors clanged to but we didn't go anywhere. Neither of them had thought to push the button.

"I think he's a little common, Ruthie," said one. After an embarrassing moment of quiet, the other one said, "Well, I guess I'm common, too."

The first one sighed. I reached around and hit the button—quite irritated—and they didn't notice, just took it for granted when we started to move.

"What are you going to do about him?" said the first one.

"Do?" said her friend as I leaped out.

I crossed the lobby, avoiding the desk as well as I could. I seated myself in the dining room, and that same girl brought me coffee and the *Herald*. There was nothing about Ironpants, and I wondered where he was keeping himself. Perhaps the women I'd come down with were his wife and sister. Maybe they'd gone out to the Moulin Rouge for their first night, and Ruthie had fallen for an acrobat.

I did see the notice for the Balmain collection, and prayed I'd be seeing it with Charles as he had promised. Or what if I had dreamed him?

I sat dreaming and eating the small brioches they brought until it was eleven and I had to go up and get ready. I did not bother to look sentimentally around at the painted girls or in other ways mark the end of my stay. I only paused in the dining room door to see that the deskman was looking the other way. I meant to run across to the stairs and duck him, in case the wire had come.

At first there appeared to be nobody back there with the clock and the surprising sign advertising the Grand Hôtel du Louvre, place du Théâtre-Français. I ran across. But then he must have popped up from below. "Ah, *mademoiselle*, a telegram has come for you this morning!"

I knew he meant me, but I looked around naïvely. He was smiling in his black suit and tie. "Good news, I hope," he said.

COME HOME ON TIME HATTIE SAYS
YOUR MOTHER

How did she hear about it? Hattie must have called her long-distance, and yet I'd never heard of such a thing in the history of my family. Later I found out that Hattie hadn't wanted to decide if I could stay without asking my parents. She'd explained it all in a night letter to New York. But to say Hattie wanted me to come straight home was not correct. I guess my mother thought saying so was a good idea. She liked to try strange methods of getting her way. I remember times I'd be dressing to go out, and she'd stand near me and mutter, "Give you a dollar if you'll wear white," or "Wonder how many you'll be sitting out?" if she wanted me to stay home.

I couldn't fight her on this, though, because Hattie would never side with me, and even Mr. Lazarus would hear about it. And all the buyers. Soon I'd be just like Willi Hanke, somebody they'd tell awful stories about in Paris. The Girl from Columbus Who Wouldn't Go Home. And Daphne Twomey would say around Weinburg's, "I saw it coming a mile off."

Back in my room again, I closed the shutters and hurled myself onto the nicely made bed. One day more.

The vapors around the bathtub were one hundred percent opaque this time, and I did feel like Hedy. Kind of tragic. This seemed just like the type of bath rich Czechs and Sudeten German women would take, according to something that was written in the Middle Ages. But only on the night before their marriage! A bath where even if all your aunts came into the room, they couldn't see you—that type of thing. I don't know where all that hot water came from, but I used it.

When I got out, I toweled my hair, and even stood for a

while with my head out the window. Tragic old Paris. It was my town! I got into my navy blue dress, leaving the jacket off and leaving my pearls off. Then I was ready. I sat down to shiver and worry about it all. I had to go. Tomorrow night I'd be back on the *Berengaria*. Only I was in love with someone, and he was on *this* side.

They called at just after twelve o'clock to say that M. de Gainsbourg was waiting for me. I was so unsettled as I left my room that I considered taking all my things with me, in case this led to running away, or—what? Going to the devil in some way, I suppose.

He was leaning against one side of the big brass doors, all dressed up. He looked at me seriously as I entered the lobby but began to smile when I was halfway to him. With his arm around me we walked out into the street—turning in the direction that led away from the place Vendôme—the one I associated with the river.

As we went along he told me I was pretty, and he hoped I didn't mind if he went with me to Balmain. I said that would be good, since I didn't know the address, and then we laughed. But instantly I felt it was a waste of our time for me to tease him. I took hold of his hand, which was on my right shoulder, and said I hoped we could go back down to the Seine sometime that day. He looked down into my face, then had to toss his hair back.

"We can go after Balmain. And see the sun . . ." He paused and then held his hand up in front of our faces. "We could see the sun just come down. . . ."

"The sunset, you mean."

"Yes. Make us forget our troubles." He waved his arm. "Everything!"

We were in the avenue George V, just in front of a vertical

TABAC sign that is no longer there. I said to him, "You haven't any troubles, Sharl."

"I have the trouble of your going away tomorrow, don't I?"

"Oh, well!" I said stupidly, "that doesn't mean anything." And here I believe I gave his arm a squeeze.

We sat down at a big café outside and ordered. A lady behind me but facing Charles called out to him, "Hello! Hello!"

"Don't turn around, Louise. Maybe she mistakes me."

Perhaps to avoid her, he stared steadily at me, and so I stared steadily back, while her calling rang in my ears. It was because I was startled and not because I was brave. But all the things that people in love want, I began to want that minute. I mean for us to be alone, to be held, to hear him say my name differently from how everybody else said it, for him to kiss me and me to kiss him back. There it went blurry. I hadn't thought about those things, but perhaps I could picture them all of a sudden. But just with him!

He leaned in to me and murmured, "Now she's coming over here."

"Well, hello there, you! Didn't you recognize me, Mr. ah— well, excuse me, but aren't you the gentleman I spoke to at Main's? At Mainbocher?"

Charles half-rose. I realized in that moment that Charles must have had a thousand girlfriends.

"No, but sit *down!*" said the woman. He did so.

"I'm sorry, *madame.*"

"Oh, I know!" she exclaimed, laughing and leaning around to look into my face to share the joke. "I merely *saw* you, and I spoke to someone else." Her voice deepened. "Yes, it was the very day Willi Hanke died—poor thing—and I was saying I thought he looked so ill! I just *felt* something, you know— something terrible. You must excuse me. And you, too!" she said to me. Then she fluttered both hands in the air and shook her head. "I must just get m'self a cab."

Charles smiled politely. She made her way out to the curb and, after standing there a moment, waved her white hankie at a surge of traffic that was just coming.

"She's still looking at you, out of the corner of her eye. Thinks I don't know it."

"I never saw her before in my life," he said.

"Maybe she loves you."

"May-be."

"Maybe you love *her*."

"Yes, may-be. Pardon."

He rattled off some words to the waiter, who eventually brought us two *gratinées* and some hard-boiled eggs and bread. We ate holding hands. We stared, too, since we'd learned how. Since Charles's manners were so correct, his staring had a big effect. Me, who was sick once for a week when I was eight, just to get out of seeing our landlord, who—I thought—had watched me coming down the stairs! But this I couldn't have hidden from. My breathing was affected. If I could have stood leaving him, I'd have gotten up and run down the boulevard screaming. Sometimes it was the expression in his eyes, but sometimes it was the way he held a cigarette in his two brown fingers. I felt that my chest was caving in.

"Will you get me some coffee with milk, please?"

He put out his cigarette and tossed his head at the waiter. The waiter nodded quickly, like a soldier who is ready to go on a mission and says to his leader, "I understand the danger."

Charles said, "I try to imagine your life in New York."

"Well, it isn't very much like this," I said, looking around at the seated people—all with their newspapers and their tiny drinks. "Most of these people would be indoors. They'd be at their offices. And if they were caught drinking at this hour, they'd be fired."

"What about the 'bar and grills'?"

"It would be only the unemployed at this hour. Even my father only goes evenings, and he doesn't have a job. But it would look wrong over there. My father goes to the Jumble Shop Bar. . . . He has to go, because my mother won't have liquor in the house."

"She is very strict?"

"She's just . . ."

"And, is it true, Louise, that New York is the largest Italian city in the world? It's . . . *incroyable*. Just look."

He pulled a little book out of his jacket pocket and handed it to me, saying, *"Cecil Beaton's New York*. Let's look for the Jumble Shop Bar. And perhaps a picture of your neighborhood. But look at this, Louise!"

He took it out of my hands and ran quickly through the pages—then thrust it back at me. There was a photo of a barbershop, very poor-looking. On the window they had painted a large, sinister, peering eye, and around it were the words "BLACK EYE SPECIALIST."

"It's the Masons," Charles whispered. "Regard how they are everywhere!"

I looked at him in surprise. Was he really afraid of the Masons—men who ate at secret lunches? Men like, say, Dan?

"My little kind of joke, Louise."

"I knew you were kidding," I replied. "I can always tell with you."

"Tell me what this guy does," he resumed, poking at the photo with his index finger. "You go in there and he hits you?"

"I don't know what it is. We don't live on the Bowery, you know."

"Oh!"

I took the book and studied it a minute. It really was incredible.

"If you get a black eye, you go to him and he covers it with makeup. I guess that's what it is."

"It's incredible, Louise. What a city!"

He leaned back in his chair and shut his eyes halfway, as he seemed often to do when he was pleased, or looking at something he was fond of. "How I would like to go to New York and get a black eye, and run down to the Bowery and get it repaired. Perhaps with the police after me!" He smiled at me. "What a country!"

"Now I s'pose you think all American men get black eyes every day."

"Yes, I do."

"You'd probably be too scared to come over and visit."

"I would like it very much," he said seriously. "And perhaps I could do some business over there."

"Bicycles?"

"No. I mean fabrics. For my father. We have talked about it. But I must stay in Paris until Philippe will come out of the army and take my place in April. But for myself I would go with you right now—tomorrow—and follow you while you travel alone. I would protect you from . . . footpads! You wouldn't know I was there until you heard the sounds of fighting. Possibly a shot . . . A man has jumped out at you, but I killed him. I will tie him up with my tie. I have a black eye but no matter! The man is Alvin Karpis! But I don't care, if you give me one smile, see."

"I see. Well, when could you come?"

He frowned slightly and pushed back his hair. "In seven months Philippe will be through his *service militaire*. Then, perhaps—if my father doesn't change his mind. But if he does, *voilà!* There is young Philippe to help him and he should not need me." He smiled sweetly and shook his head. "He knows I don't care about the business. But he can't believe it! Anyway, Louise, all this matters only if there is no war. So."

I was quite surprised by this last remark, amazing as it seems. While he put some money on the table and the book back in his pocket, I watched and waited for explanations. He just smiled at me, though, and said, "Come, *mademoiselle*. M. Balmain *nous attend.*" He shook his head as if deprecating Balmain a little bit, and I forgot his remark about the war. I was thinking, does he know Balmain, too?

What I remember of that collection—apart from the lovely walk that preceded it—was the thick carpet in a soft rose color, strewn around with tiny gilt chairs. (And yet so many of the buyers were quite heavy people.) I also recall the one silly dress I bought. Since we'd arrived a bit late, Charles was seated behind me, making me self-conscious in my reactions. I felt he mustn't see me writing anything on my *fiche* when an ugly dress came along, or just a dress I wouldn't be seen in! How silly, since he was most likely taking a nap. The result of my cowering and worry was that I bought a dress that had sleeves *and* straps. It was totally devoid of "design integrity." It was black chiffon, although the straps were satin (and only about eight inches wide!). I thought of Hattie the second I saw it coming down the aisle, and I determined to find some way of giving it to her. It only lacked a hankie with a nasturtium appliquéd on it, buttoned to the bodice with a button that didn't work.

I was so giddy at the thought that Charles might come over. I looked around at him every minute. He was always looking my way, too. By and by he leaned over and laid his arm along my chairback. I waited for a whisper but none came. It's good nothing more silly than the black chiffon dress came along. I would have bought it, just out of eagerness to ruin my old life and get on with my new one.

The salesgirl brought me a cup of tea while I arranged to pay for the dress. Of the five I had bought, this was the only one I wouldn't have worn myself. Yet I knew that if I couldn't give it to Hattie, it would be the easiest one of all to sell to Mrs. Vincent Jones or somebody. Any of those who'd come under Hattie's wing would want it because it was so fussy. I forgot to say, the bodice was some kind of funny *éponge*— means sponge—and it made you look like you'd been inflated and were only being held in by a row of black satin *x*'s that ran up the bosom from the waist—like laces on a Bavarian girl. I did give it to Hattie, but I don't believe she kept it. (But I do remember how her eyes lit up when she took it out of its tissue paper—straps, sleeves, chiffon, éponge, and all at once. It was everything a dress should be.) I was so anxious to give it to her, I had them send it to the hotel, and the next day I would take it in my luggage. The other dresses had been sent off to the docks by M. Danon. He took all the arrangements very seriously, so that my purse was bursting with receipts and bills of lading.

At four I was through. Seeing Daphne Twomey out of the corner of my eye, I moved abruptly toward the door without stopping to look for Charles, who had gone to speak to someone. I hurried through the group that stood blocking the door—most of them familiar faces by this time—and went out into pouring rain. I could just see down the street into the place Iéna. The rain was falling there also. The cars were all shiny, the umbrellas were up. Needless to say, I'd wanted to go to the river. I said, "Damn," and tried to slam the door shut. It was too heavy. I went back into the showroom. He was standing there with two men I didn't know. I took a chair

near him and to distract myself I got the New York book out
of his pocket.

I read here and there in the book, marveling that my own
city could be made to sound so odd. For example, I read:

> The general rules of behavior are rigidly adhered to, and Mrs.
> Post's book on etiquette is as strictly interpreted in Gotham as
> the Koran in Mecca. Every morning a newspaper carries an
> illustrated featured called "The Correct Thing."

I could imagine my mother sitting and reading "The Correct
Thing" at our kitchen table, but only to find something to
snort at, and she'd snort at it all day while she vacuumed.
Hattie might also read it, but she wouldn't obey it. Who
would? Of the people I knew, only Betty Wheeler's father, I
felt, supposing he decided to marry into high society.

I replaced the book, feeling intolerably restless. I wanted us
to leave and get down and see the river even in the rain. There
was no letup in their conversation—business talk about "les
Indes" and "la Perse." I was leaving him in the morning, too.

"I would like you to meet Mademoiselle Merrill," he said,
at that moment breaking into English. He touched my back,
and I stood up—not sure if that was the correct thing—and
shook hands. Very politely, they asked me if I was enjoying
my visits to the collections. They let on they'd seen me before.
Charles explained they were consultants for stores all over
Europe. I could just hear Hattie: "How do men know what
women like?"

I told Charles about the rain but that I still wanted to go
"down where we'd planned." This caused the fashion consultants to smirk.

"Better take her, Sharl, *tout de suite*, wherever it may be,"
said one of them.

Charles laughed and smiled at me, only saying, "We shall have to buy an umbrella." He shook hands with them and I snubbed them. As we walked away I thought perhaps I'd overdone it, and so I turned and waved. How foolish!

I insisted we not stop for an umbrella, so we quickly got into a cab. Charles seemed resigned to treating this as an urgent mission. He looked surprised as we rounded each corner, and puffed his cigarette.

In five minutes we were standing dead opposite the Eiffel Tower, with the river and a fancy bridge between us. It was dark for the hour. The misty, claustrophobic air, and the look of the flat gray river with the tower seeming to lie down in it, were almost too much for me. I felt sorry for the decline of all these objects I'd been dreaming about. Charles put his jacket over my head and held it on my shoulders, while I clung unhappily to the wall. The beautiful skyline of Paris—well, it made me miserable.

"Have you gone in for being sick of life, like the girls of New York City?" Charles whispered. Slowly he turned me around. His face was streaming with rain and smiling.

"I just can't say good-bye to you tomorrow," I told him. "That'll be so awful."

"We'll go take a drink with Philippe. I said we would. Tomorrow he goes back to Nîmes, and—he is so stupid you'll forget all about this rain. Forget everything sad." He pushed my hair off my face and kissed me on the lips—a real kiss. His lips seemed familiar and unfamiliar. And why familiar I don't know, because never had I been near such a beautiful man. Yes, there was Wentworth, and I'd kissed his ear. There was Harry, but Harry had always been mad. Charles was not only not mad, he was even serene and smiling as he curved over me, even if he was kissing and whispering madly.

With nobody near us because of the rain, and barely anyone

in view, there was nothing to stop us until we were too tired to stand still anymore. We stepped back and laughed at ourselves without shyness. Then every word he said went straight into my heart and memory and stayed there.

We had a long cab ride to get to where Philippe was waiting for us, so I lay against him. While he smoothed my hair back, I thought about how I was now going to the devil. But I knew I was really no different and no worse than Jean or Miss Slats and a billion other women.

As for my departure next day, I couldn't think about it. I had a feeling like that feeling when you're a child and a grown-up takes your hands and whirls you around till in the middle of a step your feet leave the ground. All you can do is laugh with joy. And then, too, I was used to having my way. I felt it would work out.

The streets were small and twisted. We made a hairpin down one and slowed down, the driver gesturing at every lighted door. Charles assured him that what we wanted was up at the corner, rue de la Santé. We came to it at last, and through the raindrops, this door proved to be smaller than the rest.

While he paid the man, Charles told me he was sorry to take me into such a dull, small place, but it was a sentimental thing of his brother's, who'd gone to college right nearby. He said that if he didn't see Philippe now, he wouldn't see him for several months.

His arm was close around me. We were not entering a normal café, but a queer, smoky room full of staring men. They stood around with tiny cigarette butts on their lips. It was a bit suspenseful, but then I heard a careless yell. Philippe was waving from the far end of the bar.

"Louise! Sharl!" he cried, as delighted and easy as if this was his own living room. "Come see this crazy thing!"

209

We walked through the men, though they never stepped aside. Some turned away from their companions to look steadily at the bodice of my dress.

Philippe was still beaming when we got through, and we had a loud reunion. His hair seemed a bit longer, but he still had on his uniform and looked only fifteen, and thin.

Soon François Foyot came out from behind a dirty velvet curtain that enclosed something like a telephone booth with a chair in it. We had another round of handshakes, and then he drew aside the curtain.

"*Regarde-moi ça!* Look at it!" He reached in and dropped a coin in the slot. "Go in!" he said cordially to me.

Charles and Philippe burst out against him, saying, "Oh, *écoute,*" and telling him he was *fou.* I jumped inside meanwhile. Charles soon joined me and, cuddled up together, we looked at the tiny screen. We watched "After the Bath," "Nude Kisses," "Electric Chair," "Chamber of Love," and "Pig Woman Under the Knife." He would cover my eyes with his hand, and I would stand up and kiss him while the machine clicked forward.

"Ah, Louise, what am I doing to you tonight?" sighed Charles when it was over.

"Well, I'd already seen 'Pig Woman Under the Knife.' "

"Ah, l'Amérique," he replied.

"You aren't sick, Louise?" Philippe called as we came out.

"*Mais elle est formidable! Formidable!*" said François enthusiastically as he led us to one of two tables. "Now let's make her drunk!"

Another bout of scolding came from Charles and Philippe, but as I was laughing, they had to drop it. Philippe said, "This fool can barely speak any English, and yet he knows sentences like that one. You're very kind to him," he concluded.

"She understands men, my friend," said François, grandly

raising one arm. "Men like me—soldiers who are hard from duty, and . . . impressive."

"And ridiculous," said Charles.

A tired-looking girl brought us beers. Philippe spoke to her, calling her "*chère* Sidonie." And when she had gone, he said quietly, "That was Sidonie."

Then he and Charles got to talking about family things. François huddled close to me, trying to get me to see a little picture on the wall above the bar. It wasn't far away but looked very tiny in the smoke. I concentrated till I could just see it was the photo of a man. François couldn't take his eyes off it, apparently. I asked him who it was.

"Il Duce, *mademoiselle*. How cute he is!"

"*Who* is it?"

"Mussolini. *Notre* Mussolini. You see, *ces hommes attardés*— these retarded people," and as he spoke he waved his arm around the bar, "they love to look on the wall and see Mussolini!"

"*Non!*" cried Charles in disbelief, twisting around to see. Then he turned on Philippe.

"What kind of place is this that you're so fond of?"

Philippe shook his head and smiled. "Don't be so serious. Take people as you find them, right, Louise? No! Claude didn't go to college—but he is a man who means well. He admires Mussolini for being strong, that's all."

"Ah," sighed Charles, leaning back and shaking his head wearily. Then he smiled and said to me, "My Louise! First 'Pig Woman Under the Knife,' now Mussolini."

"We call him 'Mr. Smith.' " murmured Philippe with a little laugh. "After all," he said looking around dramatically, "there may be Commies here."

"*Ou bien, des éclaireurs chrétiens,*" said François.

211

"Christian Boy Scouts," translated Philippe, suddenly re-turned to maturity. "By the way, Charles," he went on, "did you hear what the Duce said at his rally this week?"

François laughed.

"He said that the Abyssinians were barbarians because they . . . resisted the Italian invasion. Because they caused the deaths of Italian youths. So they deserved to die!"

We laughed, and then perhaps we realized that, after all, these people had put a picture of the man on the wall. Charles signaled for Sidonie to come with the check, and François said, *"Ah, le mauvais quart d'heure."*

"He means the bad quarter of an hour. When the check comes," said Philippe, frowning. "I am sorry we have to say good-bye this way, Louise, in talking about Mr. Smith of Italy and being like stupid boys. We can be quite dignified at times. But, anyway, it does not reflect on my brother, who is a better man in every way. Though perhaps he does not deserve a girl like you."

"Be quiet, Philippe," said Charles. *"Au revoir."* They shook hands, and François said *"Salut"* all around. I put out my cigarette and stood up. Philippe and François both came around to give me kisses on each cheek, like polite little cousins, and then they left.

It was beautiful outside, since there was a mist but no more rain. There were no cars either, so it was quiet all around. We stood on the curb holding hands, and then we kissed.

We went to the apartment where he lived with his parents. They were away in Mentone. We ate there, and then I stayed all night. No one came in to bother us.

He took me to the hotel next day—right about dawn—and waited outside as before, when Daphne Twomey had spotted him and I'd thought he was a sissy, because he was so polite.

When I'd packed and paid my bill, and been kissed by M. Danon as well as a woman I'd never seen before, we went to the station. I badly wanted him to go to Cherbourg with me, but he had two more meetings with Lelong that day that he had to attend for his father. This fact hit me hard, I remember, as I packed. But as the minutes went by, it began to seem like a small thing, compared to the overall suffering that was upon us—I mean the seven months of separation we envisioned.

We drank *chocolat* in the clanging station restaurant they had put so near to the platforms. But too soon we had to jump up and get rid of my trunk. We gave it to a porter, and he laughed at us. It made me very angry.

Charles had seemed so happy ever since we'd left Philippe's bistro the night before, and now walking to my train he did everything to make me calm and hopeful. He was even carrying my blue hat and my purse, so that I could walk with both my arms around his waist and my head on his shoulder. (Maybe that's what made the porter laugh.)

Even though I was hiding my wet eyes in his collar, I was able to see the signs for Cherbourg multiplying, and the green lacquered train that they all pointed at. I started to cry in earnest, and Charles actually said, "Perhaps you'll see Ed again. Wasn't that his name? That would be nice!"

They then passed a law: that the people in the army had to stay in the army, and men of Charles's age had to stay in France. He wrote me all the time, until that summer, when I started hearing only now and then and the letters didn't seem to be real.

In October they sank the *Athenia* on its way to New York,

213

and I realized I wouldn't see him until the war was over. But after France fell I never heard from him again. Even though his family was prominent and well-to-do, there is no record of what happened to any of them, beyond the dates when they were taken—the parents first, and then the sons.